FIONA THOMPSON HOUSE

A NOVEL

BY DAVID MENON

This is for Maddie as always with love from LBP … and it's also dedicated to Pat McDonald, the highly acclaimed Australian actress who once played the character of Fiona Thompson.

David was born in Derby, England in 1961 and has lived all over the UK but now he divides his time between Paris, where his partner lives, and the northwest of England. In 2009 he gave up a long career in the airline industry to concentrate on his writing ambitions. He's now published seven books including two series of crime novels set in Manchester, one featuring DCI Sara Hoyland and the other featuring his new detective, Jeff Barton, along with two stand alone crime mystery novels, 'Gypsy' and 'The Wild Heart' and a book of short stories with very macabre endings called 'Kind of Woman'. When he gets any spare time he teaches English to foreign students, mainly Russians. His other interests include travelling, politics, international current affairs, all the arts of literature, film, TV, theatre and music and he's a serious fan of American singer/songwriter Stevie Nicks who he calls the voice of his interior world. His loves Indian food and a glass of wine, usually red, or two.

FIONA THOMPSON HOUSE

ONE

Stephanie Marshall was a Sydneysider who'd ran her own business as a private investigator for the last ten years. Her office was in Beaconsfield on the way into the city from the airport and was on the top floor of a grey three-storey building sandwiched between a pub and a bottle shop. If word of mouth was anything to go by she'd be as rich as bloody shit. She was good at her job. She did what she said and she was reliable enough to have gained an enviable reputation in the trade. She only wished her clients could be as reliable when it came to paying her fee after she'd got them their desired result. But too many of them seemed to run short of funds when it came time to pay up and that made her cash flow situation an absolute disaster at times. But it went with the territory. She couldn't take the full fee in advance because the nature of the work meant that it was so unpredictable and she couldn't accurately forecast her costs. So it was a case of sucking it all up and hoping that at least some clients would come through the door who would end up being able to pay their invoice in one go instead of dribs and drabs.

She'd grabbed herself a coffee from the café on the corner where Ricardo the Italian owner flirted madly with her whilst his wife who also worked there laughed. She was well used to her husband taking the traditional Italian male view of the female species. Stephanie sometimes used it to her advantage though. Ricardo knew a lot of people who would talk to him and not the police and that made him a mine of useful information for her on some cases.

On the landing outside her office she caught herself in the long wall mirror. She should do something with her hair. It was the most boring shade of brown and just sat there, parted in the middle and the length catching her shoulders. She thought about maybe putting a colour on it but she had no idea what. Then there was the question of her hips. They were starting to be the first thing she saw when she looked at her body. Too many takeaway sandwiches eaten whilst conducting surveillance work were to blame for that. Too many curries, fish and chips, microwave meals, late night liquid suppers involving a bottle of Shiraz because she couldn't be bothered to do anything with food. The trousers she was wearing had room to spare six months ago. Now she could barely get her hand down the front. She was going to have to do something to arrest this particular development. Her white shirt looked alright and her black jacket was okay if she left it undone. She used to be able to click her fingers and get any man. Now if she went next door to the pub and clicked her fingers they'd probably all run for the hills. She laughed at how ridiculously deceiving human beings can be with themselves. She wasn't fat and she hadn't lost it. She just needed to lose a bit to help her get some of it back.

It was almost ten o'clock on a Wednesday morning and it was pouring with rain outside. She had someone coming to see her on the hour and when the security buzzer downstairs was activated she looked briefly at the video shot and let her visitor in, telling her over the intercom to take the lift to the third floor.

The woman who Stephanie greeted warmly at the door with a handshake had clearly been a particularly alluring beauty in her youth. She was still a very attractive woman now with her short white hair and large bewitching eyes. Stephanie would put her in her early sixties but she was preserving well and her light brown suede jacket and skirt also helped to take the years off her. She'd also taken care that her jewellery and make-up were subtle additions to her appearance and didn't overwhelm her look. She had a poise about her that told you that she could be the best friend you'd ever had but also warned you not to cross her or you'd regret it. Vulnerable, insecure and yet a hidden ferociousness that wouldn't take much to be unleashed.

'I'm Patricia Palmer' said her visitor, brightly.

'Yes, please come in, Mrs. Palmer and sit down' said Stephanie.

'Oh please call me Patricia' she said in a deep almost husky voice that told Stephanie that Patricia Palmer was either a smoker or a former smoker. She couldn't smell it on her breath but that wasn't necessarily an indication.

'And I'm Stephanie. Would you like a cup of tea or coffee?'

'No, thanks' said Patricia, smiling as she sat down in the chair in front of Stephanie's desk. 'I'm fine. It's not been long since breakfast'.

Stephanie sat down at her desk and folded her hands before resting them in front of her. 'So, Patricia, how did you find me?'

'You have a particular reputation for finding people' said Patricia. 'We saw the feature about you recently in one of the Sunday papers. That's when I decided to get in touch'.

'We?'

'Me and my husband David' Patricia explained. 'He's waiting outside in the car'.

'He's not coming in?'

'No, he prefers to let me handle this kind of thing. We have a farm in the country and he manages that'.

'I see' said Stephanie. 'So do I take it there's someone you want me to try and find?'

'Yes' said Patricia. She took a paper tissue out of her handbag and dabbed at her eyes. 'I want you to try and find a friend of mine who went missing over three years ago. He was my best friend actually and I miss him terribly'.

'Okay' said Stephanie. 'What was his name?'

'Neil Jenkins'.

'And when you say he went missing, how do you mean exactly?'

'His car was found abandoned on a quiet road near to some cliffs up at Palm Beach. The door to the drivers' side was open and the keys were still in the ignition'.

'Very mysterious' said Stephanie. 'And there was no sign of him I take it?'

'No' said Patricia. She stole herself for a moment and then carried on. 'Sorry. It's just that … well he was almost like a son to us. He was a good looking boy but obviously a lot younger than me and in any case I'm happily married to David so there was never anything like that involved'.

'How did you know him?'

'He was one of the tenants at a block of apartments I own over at Manly called Fiona Thompson House'.

'Fiona Thompson?'

Patricia smiled enigmatically. 'Fiona was an old … friend. She's dead now and I know she never thought much of me but I did have a kind of grudging respect for her. I have a resident manager at the house called Andy Green who was much closer to Fiona than I ever was. Fiona used to manage the place herself until she died and Andy took over. It was him who insisted we rename it after her'.

'So how did you become friends with Neil?'

'We met when he moved in and David and I just hit it off with him. He'd been estranged from his mother since he was little and he'd never met his father. I think perhaps that we filled those roles for him in a way, you know?'

'I do. Did he have a job?'

'Yes. At the Southern Cross bank downtown. He was a teller there'.

'Girlfriend or boyfriend?'

'Neither' said Patricia. 'When it came to personal relationships he was rather confused about himself'.

'Confused?'

'Neil was attracted to men but he didn't feel gay if that makes sense. He didn't feel part of that world and that led to a lot of confusion deep down inside him. He fell for a lot of men, all of whom were straight and of course that didn't do him any good because it led to one heartbreak after another'.

'Do you have a photograph of him?'

'Yes, of course' said Patricia. She took the photo of Neil out of her handbag and gave it to Stephanie. Neil was sitting on a chair in the back garden of her house dressed in a vest like top and shorts. He had a can of VB in his hand and he looked very relaxed.

'He's handsome' said Stephanie. 'Where does he get his dark skin from?'

'His mother was white but his father came from Syria'.

'Hence the dark eyes and black hair'.

'That's right'.

'So did he have any intimate relationships at all?'

'Oh yes, but always with straight men who had gay affairs on the side'.

'It happens'.

'But the affairs were always short lived or he wouldn't hear from them for weeks and then suddenly they'd call and he'd drop everything to see them. He let himself be used all the time but he was desperate for something romantic to work, you know? He knew that some men leave wives and girlfriends for other men and he hoped that's what would happen to him in a way. He'd never have put any pressure on a man in that way though. He'd have just been delighted if any of them had made that decision though. He'd have made a good partner for someone. He was a very caring person and he'd have had enough love for both of them if the other guy didn't feel quite as much'.

'Could he have just taken off and tried to start again somewhere else?'

'No' said Patricia, firmly. She leaned forward to make her point. 'I've gone through that over and over in my head and I really don't think that was the case. I knew Neil. I was probably closer to him than anybody. He wouldn't do that to his friends and all the people he cared about. He'd been given the cold shoulder by all of his family but he'd built his own family with his circle of friends and he wouldn't have done that to us. If he'd wanted to do that he'd have told us and planned it. He wouldn't have just taken off and left all that drama behind him'.

'Drama?'

'Abandoning his car like that'.

'But that's just what he did do'.

'But what I'm saying is that something happened to make him. He wouldn't have done it off his own back'.

'When did you last see him?'

'The night before he disappeared he came over to our place. He had dinner with David and I, we talked, we watched telly for a while and then he went home. I rang him the next day, like I rang him most days, and left him a message which I often did because he was at work. But when he didn't return it I rang him again because normally he returned my calls pretty quickly. Then I rang him again and then again and then I saw the item on the local evening news which showed his car'.

'And that's when you knew?'

'Yes. It was a terrible shock as you can imagine. I've never heard anything from him since then. Nobody has'.

'What did the police say?'

'Well they investigated but there weren't any clues for them to work with' said Patricia, her voice full of exasperation. 'The nearest houses were a kilometer away and nobody saw anything. It was as if he'd simply vanished into thin air but of course that's not possible'.

'Patricia, I have to ask you ... '

' ... suicide?' Patricia shook her head. 'No. The police thought it was suicide because of where they found the car. They thought he must've thrown himself off the cliffs in a sudden moment of absolute despair. But as mixed up as he was Neil wouldn't have done that'.

'You seem pretty certain of what he wouldn't have done, Patricia'.

'Because I knew him, Stephanie' said Patricia, intensely. 'It may have crossed his mind but he'd never have gone through with it. He wanted to be happy. He wanted to lay his demons to rest and he would've done sooner or later'.

'Not everybody finds happiness in life, Patricia'.

'No but they don't all commit suicide either' said Patricia. 'And Neil wouldn't have done. He just wouldn't'.

'Okay, well tell me more about yourself, Patricia?'

'Why?'

'To help me gain an understanding of those close to him'

'Why don't you tell me about yourself first?' Patricia asked. She preferred to gain the upper hand on someone before they gained it on her. 'Your accent is native but there's somewhere else in there?' Stephanie smiled. This lady was good. She'd successfully turned the focus away from herself. She was manipulative and there was far more to her than you'd get from any first impression. 'Well you're right my accent isn't native although I've lived here for over fifteen years. But I'm originally from the UK'.

'Do you go back very often?'

'I haven't been back since my father's funeral almost a couple of years ago'.

'I'm sorry' said Patricia.

'He'd been ill for some time' Stephanie explained. 'It was a relief to be honest'.

'I understand' said Patricia. 'So how come you were living here in the first place?'

'I moved out here from Nottingham in the East Midlands region of England with my husband and our two children for a better life like so many Brits do' Stephanie remembered. 'Two years later he moved back and I stayed here'.

'And your children?'

'They went back with their father'.

'Ouch. And it still hurts?'

'Only every day' Stephanie admitted. 'I've missed out on so much to do with them. I used to go back every year to see them but then that had to stop'.

'Why?' asked Patricia. She liked Stephanie. Beneath the veneer she thought she might be detecting the same fragility that Patricia would acknowledge about herself. She also put her in mind of her old friend Charlie Bartlett. Not that Stephanie and Charlie were alike, far from it, they were at complete opposite ends of the personality spectrum. But she felt a kind of connection with Stephanie that was almost comforting just like it had once been with Charlie. She hadn't spoken to Charlie in years. That was one relationship she hadn't been able to mend. Charlie had cut her off all those years ago and she'd never shown any signs of putting what Patricia had done behind them. She still missed her sometimes though and wondered what Charlie was up to now. They'd been through so much together back in the day.

'My ex-husband remarried and his new wife thought it was unsettling to have me turn up every year' Stephanie explained. 'You know what it's like with some second wives. They have to make their mark and damn the consequences for everybody else. I wanted to fight it but I didn't have the money and my ex-husband had legal custody. Besides, my kids didn't want to come back to Australia'.

'Why did your husband go back without you?'

'Because I was having an affair'

'Ah. So that's why you stayed?'

'Yes' said Stephanie. 'And God I put myself through it over that decision'.

'Everybody judged you as a bad mother, right?'

'Oh I was the wicked witch from Hell even as far as my own parents were concerned. I was hoping though that my children would grow up to hate their step-mother more for refusing to let me see them than they hated me for staying out here. But they've shown no signs of it yet. I have two boys, James and Matthew. James is taking a gap year soon before going to university and I'm hoping he'll come down here to see his old Mum. I'd be so happy if he did. Anyway, it sounds like you know a thing or two about this sort of thing?'

'Oh believe me I wrote the book on screwed up relationships between mothers and children' said Patricia. 'And I do know what it's like when it feels like the whole world is judging you for it. I have twins, John and Angela. They live up in Queensland and run a hotel together in Port Douglas with Angela's husband Rob. John doesn't have any children but Angela and Rob have got three. I see them from time to time and one of my grandsons is at university here in Sydney so we see him a fair amount which is lovely. He seems to like his grandma and granddad and we've become good mates. What complicates things slightly is that Rob is the brother of my husband David's first wife Beryl'.

'Phew'.

'I know. We're a complicated lot and I wasn't always sure that David and I would end up together. We went through a hell of a lot in the early days and we both wasted far too many years married to other people. But you can't fight your destiny and we've been together now for over twenty years'.

'True love?'

'Well yes, I think it is true love' said Patricia, smiling broadly. She worshipped the ground David walked on. She always had done. 'But what about you? Are you with anyone now?'

'No' said Stephanie who quite envied Patricia's position in her personal life. She'd love to have some family round her and it had been a while since she'd even been out with anyone. She didn't like being on her own. 'I'm between men as they say'.

'It didn't work out with the man you stayed here for?'

'We were happy for a few years but I'd had a difficult time with Matthew's delivery and couldn't have anymore children. He said it didn't matter to him and he was happy just with me. Then he had an affair with a girl he worked with who subsequently became pregnant and all of a sudden being a father meant everything to him. So he left me for her'.

'We women can be held to ransom by our wombs' said Patricia. 'The mother of my second husband Stephen said she'd cut him out of her will unless I produced a child for him. But she knew that I couldn't have anymore children. So when she died she didn't leave us a cent'.

'Second husband? How many have you had?'

'Three, including David and I've really put him through it at times, I can tell you'.

'Well let's keep that for another time' said Stephanie. 'Now tell me, did Neil get on as well with David as he did with you?'

'Oh yes' said Patricia. 'He was close to us both'.

'And do all of his friends believe as you do that he didn't take off for somewhere else or commit suicide?'

'Yes, they all absolutely do agree with me' said Patricia. 'Stephanie, something happened to Neil that night. I want to know what that was. I miss him. I miss his laughter and I want him back in our lives'.

'I'll do my best, Patricia. It isn't encouraging that the police didn't come up with anything but maybe I can be more fortunate. I'll do some preliminary research and then I'll be back to you for some more details'.

Stephanie went through her fees and Patricia paid the deposit with her bank card.

'Would you say that Neil was happy when he disappeared?' Stephanie asked.

'No, but deep down he was never happy. He was a tortured soul. But he was desperate to belong and he did belong with us and the rest of his friends'.

'And he gave no indication that anything like this would happen?'

'No' said Patricia. 'None of it makes any sense at all, Stephanie. None of it'.

Patricia walked briskly to where David's car was parked a little way down the street. He looked up from doing the crossword in the morning paper when Patricia got in.

'How did that go?' he asked.

'Pretty well, I think' said Patricia. 'She seems very capable and quite understanding. I really quite liked her'.

'Did you tell her the real reason why you want to find Neil?'

Patricia couldn't believe he'd actually asked her that. 'David, finding Neil could mean the answer to all our problems'.

'So you didn't tell her'.

'No I didn't tell her, David! And there's no reason for her to know'.

'I haven't seen this side of you for a long time, Pat' said David in his usual quiet way that signaled disapproval. 'I thought all these games were well behind us'.

'David, I haven't been pushed into a corner like this for a long time and it's not a very comfortable place to be, let me tell you. But I'm doing this for the both of us, David. Don't you ever forget that'

'Oh I won't, Pat, I won't. But that's what scares me the most. I know more than anybody what you're capable of'.

FIONA THOMPSON TWO

Driving over the Sydney Harbour Bridge heading for the Northern beaches, Stephanie was reminded of one of the advantages of having stayed in Australia. She had the top down on her car and the view from the bridge with the opera house to the right combined to make one of the most iconic landmark images of the entire southern hemisphere. She had her sunglasses on. They were so big they covered the upper half of her face. It was a stunningly beautiful day. The light wind was blowing through her hair. She felt good. The summer had taken hold of the Sydney weather at last. Spring had been awful but now the sky was blue. These were also the moments when she missed having her sons James and Matthew with her. They were both young men now and she wondered if either of them might be dating. It would surprise her if they weren't. They were both good looking and way past the spotty early teen stage. It wouldn't bother her if they were dating girls or boys as long as they were happy and having fun. If she could pass on one mission to her sons it was that life was for living and every day was precious. It wasn't about mortgages and chasing every cent so you could keep up with whoever was living next door because those kind of people aren't really living. They're just victims of suburbia and the expectations of the middle class. Stephanie would admit to having made some mistakes. But she'd also claim she'd done her best to make up for them. And she'd also say that, despite the pain inside, it was always better to laugh than to cry.

It would be Christmas in a couple of months and she'd been planning to accept the standing invitation of the same friends she went to every Christmas Day. She knew she'd have a good time there. She had done for all the previous years. But this year she felt the ET urge to go home. So she'd gone on the internet last night and, amazingly enough, she'd found that there were still deals to be had for flights back home at the Christmas peak season. So she'd booked herself a ticket from Sydney to Dubai on December 20th with an onward connection straight to Birmingham. She'd then called her brother Colin who said he'd be delighted to pick her up from the airport and then she'd called her Mum who'd burst into tears of joy when she told her that her eldest was coming home for Christmas. Within an hour the entire festive season had been worked out. Stephanie was one of five. She had two sisters and two brothers who all had kids so there were a lot of people to get round and catch up with. But both she and her Mum were hoping that James and Matthew would be joining them this year for at least part of the festive celebrations.

But what if that didn't end up happening? What if a journey halfway round the world to try and re-connect with her sons ended up in a series of excuses and phone calls but no actual physical contact? Would she end up flying back to Sydney in January feeling even more lost than she did now? She'd sent them both emails to let them know she was coming. Neither of them had replied yet but it was only a few hours ago. She shouldn't get too anxious yet.

She found the address in Manly without too much difficulty with the aid of her little satellite machine and she pulled up outside Fiona Thompson House. It was very typical of the architecture in this area that was made up mainly of large detached houses with views that reached across the city because of their position on a hill that climbed up from the sea. There was a large gate attached to a fence that covered the front of the house. It seemed like a quiet neighbourhood. Not much was going on at eleven in the morning. A couple of cars went up and down the street. It wasn't on a bus route. It was a good five minute walk to the nearest underground station. But she could still see why people would rent a room here. It was a good address and the view was well worth it.

She went through the gate and up the path towards the front door. She stopped to look around and then heard a voice call out to her.

'Can I help you?'

She turned round to see a tall man walk round the corner from the side of the house. He was bathed in the shadow of the trees that filled the front garden and went up the side but when he emerged into the sunlight Stephanie was immediately struck by his smile. It was slightly cheeky and yet self-conscious at the same time. His hair was going thin on top and he was wearing one of those dark blue all in one thick cotton overalls with pockets everywhere that men like car mechanics and electricians wear. So which one was he? It had a zip up the front and it was open enough for Stephanie to see he had a healthy looking rug on his chest. She liked what she saw. She felt herself smiling. She'd always had a taste for working man crumpet. So-called intellectuals and professionals tended to spend more time up their own backsides than anywhere else. She was attracted to rawness. He reached round and scratched the back of his neck with his finger. It just seemed like one of those moments.

'I should introduce myself' said Stephanie.

'Well that would be a start'.

'I'm Stephanie Marshall' she said. 'I'm an investigator'.

'And I'm Wayne Hamilton' said Wayne who was enjoying the moment as much as Stephanie. He felt that lurch in his stomach when she set her eyes on him. He managed to reach out and they shook hands with each other. 'So what are you investigating?'

'Do you live here, Wayne?' Stephanie asked. She wished she'd worn that shorter skirt she'd hesitated over that morning when she was getting dressed. Mind you that might've made her hips look wider.

'Yes' Wayne answered. 'And I work here too. I'm the maintenance man. Well for this and a few other properties across the city'.

'Hence the working gear?'

'Yeah, look, is there anything I can help you with?'

'I don't know' said Stephanie. 'Until we start talking'.

'Well I was just going to break for a coffee. Would you like one whilst you tell me what it is you're investigating? My place is just at the back on the ground floor. We could sit outside if you feel more comfortable?'

Stephanie smiled. 'Do you always act on your impulses?'

'No' said Wayne. 'I don't actually'.

'Okay, Wayne' said Stephanie who was feeling flattered. 'Lead the way'.

'I've only got instant if that's okay?' asked Wayne, anxiously. He was shy around women he found attractive these days. When he was younger his relationships only ever led to trouble, sometimes it was his fault and sometimes it was other people interfering to ruin his life for their own reasons. Now, in his early fifties, it was as if he was starting all over again. And sometimes that felt good. But at other times it felt like a hell of a weight he had to carry.

'Instant is fine, Wayne'.

'Good' he said, smiling. 'Good'.

It was a perk of her job that sometimes in the course of an investigation Stephanie stumbled across a bit of something that would provide for some entertainment along the way. She watched Wayne's bum moving in his all in one work suit as he walked along and she had that fluttering feeling in her stomach that this might just be one of those occasions. It had been a while since she'd felt a spark with a man. She'd almost forgotten how good it did feel.

Wayne brought two mugs of coffee out to a small table round the back of the house. Stephanie had said she wanted hers black and Wayne had added a splash of milk to his own. He rather awkwardly placed an already open packet of chocolate digestive biscuits down on the table too.

'Sorry, I should've put those on a plate or something'.

'It doesn't matter' said Stephanie as she sat in one of the wicker chairs Wayne had brought over from the corner of the garden. He sat in the other one. 'I take it you don't get many visitors?'

'Is it that obvious?'

'Maybe I'll put it down to being part of your charm' said Stephanie who then took a first sip of her coffee. She couldn't stand coffee snobs. It was one of those things people used to try and say they were used to such a superior lifestyle.

'Is that okay?' Wayne asked.

'It's fine' Stephanie answered.

'So, are you going to tell me what it is you're investigating?'

'I'm looking into the disappearance of a man called Neil Jenkins' said Stephanie. 'He used to live here apparently. Did you know him?'

'No but I know of him' Wayne replied. 'He was a good friend of Andy's. Oh that's Andy Green who runs this place on behalf of the owner. Like me he looks after several sites so he isn't here at the moment I'm afraid. I am expecting him back shortly though if you don't mind waiting?'

Stephanie smiled. 'I don't mind at all'.

'I was hoping you'd say that'.

'So you didn't know Neil Jenkins?'

'No, I never met him. I came to live here about six months after he'd disappeared'.

'And what do people say about Neil Jenkins? How do they describe him?'

Wayne sat back and thought for a moment. 'Warm hearted, generous, funny'.

'An all round top bloke?'

'Yeah, but he could also be a bit moody by all accounts'.

'Oh?'

'Yeah, I think he liked his own company as much as he liked other people's'.

'That's not unusual' said Stephanie.

'Well no I'm a bit like that myself' admitted Wayne. 'Although I'm open to someone changing all that'.

'You don't miss a trick'.

'I know and yet I'm a little out of practice'.

'Don't tell me. You're newly divorced after decades of marriage and you're still finding your feet in the whole dating thing?'

Wayne flushed with embarrassment. How was he going to tell her that he'd been in prison for over twenty years for murdering Susan? It didn't exactly slide effortlessly into a conversation and since he came out of prison it had held him back from forming any relationships with women. And yet he was lonely. He was desperately lonely. His father Gordon had died whilst he was in prison and his step-mother Beryl wouldn't have anything to do with him. He had a step-brother called Robert who was now running the business Wayne's father had left behind, and which Wayne's investment had once saved, but Wayne didn't care about any of that. It was the obsession with business and money and power and revenge that had screwed him up so much when he was younger. Now all he wanted was a quiet life where nobody bothered him and he didn't bother anybody else. But he did want to share the remaining twenty or thirty years of his life with a woman who he could have a straight forward and honest relationship with. Easy to say but it meant having to tell her about his past and that's why he'd backed off before since coming out of prison. But he needed a woman. He needed the taste, the smell, the feel of a woman sleeping next to him at night.

'Well you're right about finding my feet' said Wayne, nervously.

Before Wayne could summon the courage to deal with his moment of anxiety the main gate opened and Andy Green drove his car onto the drive. He saw the attractive looking woman sitting with Wayne and went over to introduce himself.

'Are you looking for a room, Stephanie?' Andy asked. 'Only it just so happens I've got number nine available at the moment'.

'I don't need a room, Andy' said Stephanie as she looked up at the dark blond haired man with the green eyes. He wasn't ugly and looked smartly casual in his open necked shirt and jacket but he certainly wasn't having the same effect on her that Wayne had. 'I need information'.

'I'm going to leave you to it' said Wayne as he stood up. 'I'll see you before you go, Stephanie'.

'Okay, Wayne and thanks'.

Stephanie then explained to Andy that she was investigating the disappearance of Neil Jenkins.

'Neil' said Andy. 'Yeah that was all a very bad business'.

'How do you mean exactly?'

'Well Neil was a mate and he was a good mate. I've raised a daughter on my own and it's been hard at times although she really has turned out to be a great kid, thank God. But Neil was always there during the dark times, you know? He was never just a fair weather friend like so many of the phonies you meet in life'.

'But I understand he was a pretty complex character?'

'Yeah, well he felt like none of the pieces of his life fitted. He liked guys but he didn't feel gay. He liked girls but he didn't feel like he belonged in a relationship with a girl'.

'Complex indeed'.

'And yet he never wanted anything from you except for the acceptance of him as an individual. He never got that from any of his family although I've got my own thoughts about why that was'.

'Oh?'

'Well I believe his family rejected him because he was dozens of levels above them all intellectually'.

'He was bright'.

'He was more than bright. He was one of the most intelligent guys I've ever met and I don't think they could handle that. So they pushed him away like he didn't matter to them and it all started with his mother. She married his step-father even though he'd rejected Neil because he was mixed race. His maternal grandmother brought him up and it was when she died that he moved in here'.

'Was he happy here?'

'Yeah' said Andy. 'Living here was one of the few things that did make him happy'.

'If he was so intelligent why did he carry on working as a bank teller?'

'Because he spent his life looking for the key to his existence' said Andy. 'That's what was most important to him and when he'd found that he'd be able to deal with everything else. But look, why are you investigating him? Who's hired you and why?'

'Your boss Patricia has hired me'.

'Is that right?'

'Why the look, Andy?'

'Well look, Patricia is my boss but I've also known her for a very long time and believe me, that woman never does anything unless she has a very specific reason for it'.

'Are you saying it's inconceivable that she just wants to find her friend who went missing in very dramatic circumstances?'

'Yes' said Andy. 'She'll have her own reason for wanting to know now at this minute, Stephanie. I mean, she's had three years to hire an investigator to look into what happened to him. But why has she waited until now?'

Stephanie thought about what Andy was saying and wondered what ulterior motive Patricia could have for wanting to find Neil now. She'd seemed so genuine when she'd come to see her in the office. Just why was Andy so suspicious of Patricia?

'And' Andy went on. 'Neil had fallen out with Patricia shortly before he disappeared. They weren't on speaking terms'.

'Is that right?'

'Oh yes' said Andy. 'Look, I think it would be good if you went to see my daughter. She's a police officer and she'll be able to dig out the file on Neil's disappearance'.

'A police officer? No wonder you said she'd turned out to be a really good kid'.

'I'm very proud of her' said Andy who then took a card out of his wallet with his daughter's phone number on it and handed it to Stephanie.

'I'll bet' said Stephanie as she read the card and noted the address of the police station where Andy's daughter worked. 'Constable Maddy Green of the New South Wales police. Maddy? Is that short for Madeleine?'

'No, it's short for Madonna. I was a big fan in the eighties when she was born'.

'Why have you brought her up alone, Andy?'

'We haven't seen her mother since the day she left when Maddy was only a few months old'.

'Another one who just fell off the face of the earth?'.

'You could put it like that, yes. I haven't thought about her for a long time'.

'Did you see Neil on the day he disappeared?'

'Yes' said Andy. He lowered his head as if in shame. 'But only briefly. I was seeing someone at the time and I was on my way out the door to meet her when Neil came home. He looked troubled and preoccupied and I've kicked myself every day since for not stopping to ask what was wrong. But I was in a hurry. I was already late. I said I'd see him later'.

'You weren't to know what was going to happen, Andy'.

'No but it's one of those if only I'd stopped kind of things, you know'

'Yes, I do' said Stephanie. 'What do you think happened to Neil, Andy?'

'God, I've asked myself this over and over again. I don't know what happened but I do think he's alive somewhere'.

'What makes you think that?'

'In the few weeks before he disappeared he was meeting someone on a regular basis but he wouldn't say who and I never saw him with anyone. He just said that this person was helping him put some of his pieces together'.

'What did that mean?'

'I don't know because he said he was keeping it all to himself until he could tell the whole story. But he was excited and he was happy. I just don't know who it was who was making him feel that way'.

FIONA THOMPSON THREE

Patricia and David were having breakfast on the balcony of their Darling harbour apartment. It was where they stayed when they were in the city and on a bright, sunny day like it was today the temptation to sit and marvel at the view was almost too much to avoid. But after putting out the juice, coffee and toast, Patricia returned straight to the headlines in the Sydney Morning Herald.

'I think it's wonderful that the coalition has finally returned to power' said Patricia.

'Why is it so wonderful?' asked David.

'Because we've now got a government that's on the side of business' said Patricia. 'No more handouts to the lazy and no more soft touch for asylum seekers'.

'The lucky country'.

'David, we're overwhelmed'.

'Pat, we're a country of twenty-three million people in a land mass the size of Europe. It would take centuries for us to be overwhelmed. If Australia wants to be taken seriously as one of the big boys in the world then we have to take our responsibilities seriously to those in need. And besides, we're talking about thousands of people wanting to make the journey to the other side of the world. There are conflict situations elsewhere where millions of people are turning up on the borders of countries that are ill equipped to cope'.

'Yes, well you've always had a bleeding heart. It started with Beryl'.

'I'll treat that remark with the contempt it deserves'

'I thought you would'.

'Pat, the coalition built their campaign on the perception that the ALP had done nothing when that was blatantly untrue. They won an election on lies, Pat'.

'Well for once they'll be putting Australia first, second, and third every single time'.

'Now I know why you're so attracted to the idea of the Abbott government. In that last statement just replace the word Australia with Patricia'.

'And you wouldn't have me any other way'.

David smiled at her. 'No, I wouldn't but that's not to say I'll agree with you on everything'. He remembered the day over twenty-five years ago when he'd turned up at the awful motel Patricia was staying at after he'd read the notice in the paper that she'd filed for bankruptcy. He'd always known that despite her desperate, manipulative ways she'd always be the only woman for him and he hadn't been surprised when it turned out that she hadn't actually needed rescuing. It had all been an act to fool some of her creditors. She'd stashed thousands of dollars offshore which she'd managed to escape the attention of the bankruptcy regulators. So he stood by her and she started again, this time doing everything above board and without the recourse to her ways of old. They got married and settled down and in the years since they'd been incredibly happy. But now he was nervous. Patricia had always handled their finances and they'd built up quite a portfolio of the farm, the apartment, several properties in both Sydney and Melbourne that they rented out and various other stocks and shares. But now they were being investigated by the tax authorities who'd threatened to freeze all their assets. Why now?

'I've always known that, David' said Patricia. 'But you've also known that I can't live without money'.

'You mean you can't live without a lot of money, Pat, there's a difference'.

Patricia was feeling awkward. She always came up against the brick wall of David's absolute reasonableness whenever she was scheming about something. She couldn't bear to lose. She had to win. She had to come out on top. David had always known that but he still tried to rein her in. That's why she loved him so much. He was the only one who'd ever been able to do that and survive on the positive side of her feelings.

'David, you wouldn't leave me, would you?'

David looked her squarely in the eye. 'You know I wouldn't leave you, Pat. Where did that come from?'

'I just got scared'.

'Pat, I love you and besides, we've come too far and been through too much for me to even think about doing that'.

Patricia smiled. 'Thank you, darling. I could take anything except you leaving me'.

'Well you can forget all about that but look, I don't understand why the tax authorities are interested in us in a hostile way? You have played fair dinkum with them, haven't you Pat?'

'Yes, David, I have'.

'So why are they doing it?'

'The most likely explanation is that somebody tipped them off for malicious reasons'.

'About what if you've played by the rules?'

'A tip-off is enough for them to launch an investigation, David'.

'But they're threatening to close us down?'

'Whoever did tip them off must've given them some pretty devastating information'.

'And surely you can't think that Neil did that?'

'He was pretty angry with me, David. I think he's been laying low these past three years until he saw his chance to get back at me. The big dramatic show with the car was all cover to make it look like something really bad had happened to him'.

'No, Pat, I don't buy it. I don't buy it at all. We knew the bloke. He was our friend, Pat. He ate at our table, he slept under our roof. No matter how angry he was at you and I know you two had your tiffs, he wouldn't do that to us'.

'It wasn't just a tiff, David'.

'He got hold of the wrong end of the stick, that's all'.

'David, he thought I was trying to steal his money!'

'Yeah, like I said, he got hold of the wrong end of the stick but he would've calmed down. He wouldn't have put his whole life on hold for three years just to get back at you for some crazy misunderstanding over money. Pat, you're putting two and two together and making a hundred and bloody ten. And, dare I say, you're acting as if everybody is capable of being like you used to be'.

'Finished?'

'For now'

'Well do you have any better ideas than believing Neil has waited three years before striking back at me, David?'

'No' David conceded. 'I don't'.

'Well if the light does go on and you suddenly know it couldn't be Neil who's trying to ruin me then let me know. I'll be all ears'.

Stephanie was waiting in the reception area of the police station for Andy Green's daughter Maddy. Their appointment was for eleven and it was already twenty past but Stephanie didn't mind sitting there with her own thoughts. She was having her first date with Wayne later and she was looking forward to it. It had been a while since she'd been out with anyone but although the physical attraction she had for him made her want to jump on his bones straight away she'd decided she was going to be cautious and wait until the second date before she tried to seduce him. Of course if he tried to make a move on the first date then she wouldn't try and stop him. That would be rude. And anyway, neither of them were kids and she couldn't stand women of a certain age who wanted to be treated like ladies when they'd been round the track more times than an Olympic gold medal winner. Women should be honest about wanting men to get inside them and do the business. That's what sex was all about for women.

When Maddy pitched up Stephanie was struck by how pretty she was. The police officer's uniform didn't do much for her like it didn't do much for any woman but she had her father's dark blond hair and bright green eyes and a wide smile that lit up her face. She led Stephanie into a small interview room and placed a large file on the desk between them.

'Thank you for agreeing to see me, Maddy' said Stephanie. 'I know how busy you are'.

'Well my Dad said you seemed alright and he's usually a good judge of character' said Maddy.

'In my job I rarely get the red carpet laid out for me but your Dad seems like a good bloke'.

'Yeah, he is'.

'You must be close considering he brought you up by himself?'

'We are close' said Maddy. 'I'm going to miss him next year to be honest'.

'How do you mean?'

Maddy raised her hand and flashed her engagement ring. 'I'm getting married next April so I'll be moving out'.

'Oh congratulations' said Stephanie looking brightly at Maddy's ring. 'Who's the lucky man?'

'His name is Ralph and he's a police officer too'.

'And you're nuts about him?'

Maddy smiled. 'Just a bit'.

'It's written all over your face'.

'I'd like Dad to meet someone too' said Maddy. 'He hasn't lived like a monk, if a daughter is allowed to say that about her Dad, but he deserves to, you know, share his life with a good woman who'll appreciate him'.

'You never hear from your mother?'

'She's not my mother. She's the woman who gave birth to me but she's never been my mother because she was too busy putting drugs before me or Dad. I've never heard from her and I never want to'.

'Clearly, you're a young woman who knows her own mind'.

'You'd better believe it' said Maddy. 'But look, we digress. You want to know about the investigation into the disappearance of Neil Jenkins, right?'

'Yes' Stephanie confirmed.

'Well you're in luck in an ironic sort of way' said Maddy, opening the file. 'Because there's been a development in the case'.

'Oh?'

'Last week a body was found less than a kilometer away from where Neil's car was discovered. It was badly decomposed but tests have been carried out and the results have come back this morning'.

'Is it Neil Jenkins?'

'No' said Maddy. 'It isn't Neil. The body is that of a woman. All we know about her so far is that she's not Caucasian but her exact ethnic origins have yet to be determined'.

'But how is this linked to Neil Jenkins?'

'That's what the results of the tests are all about' Maddy went on. 'DNA from the body matches that found all over the passenger seat side of Neil's car. It couldn't be identified at the time but now we know that whoever that woman was she was in Neil's car'.

'Do you know how she died?'

'Yes' said Maddy. 'She was shot. The tests have found evidence of two gunshot wounds'.

'But how come the body has remained hidden for the last three years?'

'The body had been buried in a shallow grave quite a distance from any residential housing. But all the heavy rain we've been having over the winter has basically washed enough of the soil away to expose part of it. Some local kids noticed it and one of their parents rang us'.

'So what is the official line that you, the police, are taking on this?'

Maddy wiped her hand across her face. 'This is difficult for me, Stephanie, because of course I knew Neil. I knew him well and I liked him a lot'.

'What are you saying?'

'That officially this could lead to us suspecting Neil of the murder of this woman'.

'I can see how hard that would be when you knew Neil so well'.

'Which is why I probably won't be part of any further investigation because my superiors know that Neil was a friend of mine'

'How would you describe Neil's relationship with Patricia and David Palmer?'

Maddy sat back in her chair. 'David Palmer is a kind of what you see is what you get kind of guy, you know. But Patricia … she's a whole bunch of different women wrapped up in one skin and you never know which one of her is going to turn up at any given time. But Neil was a very loyal friend and he always defended Patricia from her detractors. That was until the last couple of days before he disappeared. He'd fallen out with her but neither me nor my Dad knew why'.

'Do you like Patricia?'

'Like is the wrong word' said Maddy. 'My Dad is always suspicious of her because he's known her a long time and knows what she can be like. I don't dislike her. She can be great company, she certainly looks after her appearance and she's obviously very sharp minded when it comes to business. But I wouldn't trust her and I wouldn't make her a confidant of mine'.

Stephanie was beginning to wonder just what she'd taken on with this case. It was opening up in different directions all the time. Neil Jenkins seemed like a complex character but it was Patricia Palmer who was emerging from every stone she unturned.

'Your Dad said Neil was seeing someone just before he disappeared but he was keeping tight lipped about it' said Stephanie. 'Could it have been this woman who's been found?'

'I don't know. I mean, I didn't think he liked women in that way' said Maddy, her face contorted slightly with anxiety as if she wasn't sure what she should say. 'But those last few weeks before he disappeared he did seem happy. He seemed much more together that he'd done for a long time so it could've been her who'd been putting the smile on his face. It is possible. I mean these days sexuality isn't a settled thing for some people and it certainly wasn't for Neil'.

Stephanie laughed. 'Yes. The amount of cases I've taken on from people who've suspected their husband or wife of having an affair and it turns out they were having an affair but with someone of the same sex. Most of the time they don't see that particular brick wall coming'.

'I guess it would be a bit of a surprise' said Maddy. 'But I'm not judging'.

'No of course not but back to Neil, if he was seeing this woman as in seeing her as a girlfriend, then why didn't he tell anybody about it? Why did he just give out hints about someone who was putting his pieces together?'

'That is something I don't know' said Maddy. 'But if the police come to believe that Neil was responsible for the death of this woman and then absconded to save his skin then it means that none of us really knew Neil. Not my Dad, not me, not Patricia or David, not anybody who called him a friend'.

Patricia marched into Stephanie's office. She couldn't believe who she'd just seen coming out as David drove up and parked.

'And good morning to you I'm sure' said Stephanie who was arranging the flowers Wayne had bought her in a vase. They'd been out for a few drinks the night before and they'd had a lovely time. He was the first man Stephanie had met in a long time who she really wanted to get to know. The flowers had been a wonderful surprise and tonight they were going out for something to eat after having a drink or two at his place. He'd been an absolute gentleman last night. She hoped he wouldn't be tonight though. She was well up for it.

'Was that Wayne Hamilton I just saw leaving here?'

Stephanie felt herself stiffen. 'And that's any of your business because?'

'How do you know him?'

'I'm not going to answer that question. Anyway, why do you want to know?'

'Let's just say that Andy Green gave him a place to live and a job at Fiona Thompson House against my better judgment'.

'Does he pay his rent on time?'

'Yes he does but … '

' … and does he throw wild parties that disrupt the whole neighbourhood and the police end up having to be called?'

'No'.

'Then what is your problem with him?'

Patricia stood and looked at Stephanie. Clearly there was some kind of personal connection going on between her and Wayne that she'd have to do something about because she didn't want Wayne encroaching on her business. He'd tried to destroy her before and he could easily try again.

'Do you know what?' said Stephanie, holding up her hand. 'Don't answer that because there are other things I need to know from you, Patricia. Like, why didn't you tell me you'd fallen out with Neil Jenkins shortly before he disappeared?'

'We didn't fall out'.

'That's not what others say'.

'Oh I suppose you've been listening to the long queue of people who'd love to see my face in the dirt!'

'That's a pretty big persecution complex you've got there, Patricia'.

'I have a lot of experience of being let down by weak and inferior people, believe me. You see, I'm not liked by some because I'm strong and I'm assertive. I don't suffer fools'.

'Then don't take me for one'.

'Excuse me, could I remind you just who is working for who here?'

'Oh and there's some pretty deep anger and even resentment. I'm guessing it goes a long way back?'

'I'm not here to talk about my past. I'm here because of that body they've found near Neil's car and what impact it has on the investigation? You remember? The thing I'm paying you to do? Yes, I'm passionate about what I do and I flare when I see fit so don't start going all bloody PC on me!'

'I'm not a PC kind of person'.

'I'm glad to hear it'.

'Being forthright is a virtue as far as I'm concerned'.

'So we agree'.

'So what are you hiding from me, Patricia?'

Patricia swung round on her. 'I beg your pardon?'

'Why do you want to find Neil?'

'I've told you already'.

'Yes, but now I want the truth'.

Patricia slumped down in the chair and decided to go for the haunted emotional approach. Once Neil had been found she would deal with him in her own way. Now was the time to lay it on a bit thicker than she would do normally.

'I don't have many friends, Stephanie. I never have had. People find me too intense. I know that sometimes I can go over the top. It's why my children are not exactly in regular contact. David is the only one who can handle me and really understand me and without him I'd have been lost a long time ago and God knows where I'd be now. I wanted so much to help Neil. He was wasted in that bank and he knew it. I wanted him to realise his full potential but as usual, instead of just helping I tried to completely take over his life and steer it in the direction that I thought it should go instead of listening to him and where he wanted to go. He was a grown man who could take his own decisions but he said I was suffocating him and he couldn't breathe because I was on his back the whole time. I just want to tell him that I'm sorry, Stephanie'.

'So you weren't on good terms when he disappeared?'

'No, we weren't'.

'So why didn't you tell me that at the outset?'

Patricia was crying. 'I didn't want you to think badly of me'.

Stephanie came round to the front of her desk and perched on the edge. She handed Patricia a paper tissue. She didn't know if Patricia was telling the truth or not but she had to give her the benefit of the doubt so they could move on.

'Patricia, do you know who the woman was who was in Neil's car that night? The woman whose body they've found?'

Patricia shook her head. 'No. What are the police saying about her?'

'Well they haven't been able to identify her yet but they do know she was shot and so far Neil is the only suspect'.

'But there's no way Neil could've killed anybody'

'Well if it wasn't him then who was it?'

'How would I know that?'

'But didn't you know about this mysterious person Neil was supposed to be seeing in the weeks before he disappeared?'

'No, I didn't, he didn't tell me or David about whoever it was'.

'Well I'm going to go up to Palm Beach tomorrow to look at the place where the car was found' said Stephanie. 'I need to get a view of it for myself'.

'What are your thoughts now?'

'I don't know' Stephanie admitted. 'I'm keeping a very open mind for now'.

'Including whether or not Neil could've killed that woman?'

'I have to for now, yes'.

'I'm sorry for getting upset'.

Stephanie waved her hand through the air dismissively. 'No need to apologise'.

'But Stephanie, I don't know what it is you're getting into with Wayne Hamilton but there are things about him that you need to know'.

'Well I don't expect you'll be happy until you tell me so you'd better get it off your chest'.

'Stephanie, I'm not doing it to cause trouble, I'm doing it because I like you and you should know who you're dealing with'.

'Alright, Patricia, just … tell me'.

'Wayne was my step-son'.

'What?'

'He's the son of my first husband Gordon who sadly died a few years ago. Gordon was a good man but I never loved him, not really. I married him because he was rich, he was there, and he seemed to love me'.

'Well that's honest if nothing else'.

'David and I weren't together or even in contact at the time. Gordon's first wife had died and Wayne was a young child'.

'It must've made quite a little family with your twins John and Angela?'

'I … I only had Angela with me then. John was with David'.

'How come?'

Patricia thought hard and she thought carefully. 'Let's just say that the explanation for that is a story that can wait. But has Wayne told you why nobody saw him for over twenty years?'

'No?'

'He was in prison for murder'.

The news hit Stephanie like a slab of concrete aimed directly at her chest. 'Say that again?'

'He murdered his wife Susan Hamilton' said Patricia. 'They were what you'd call estranged at the time but her maiden name was Palmer. She was David's daughter'.

FIONA THOMPSON FOUR

Wayne had changed his shirt three times in the hour before Stephanie was due to arrive and they were the only three shirts he possessed. His mate Andy Green had been teasing the life out of him but Wayne was getting seriously stressed. He wanted everything to be just right and he refused Andy's offer of a drink to calm him down. He didn't want Stephanie turning up and being able to smell alcohol on his breath. He'd showered twice and brushed his teeth half a dozen times. He felt like some stupid teenager on a first date. But the fact was he'd wanted Stephanie from the moment he saw her. Lightening had struck and gone right through his heart. And it really was making him feel like a teenager.

He had the smallest apartment in Fiona Thompson house but he liked it. It was on the ground floor at the back of the house and consisted of one room with a kitchen, bedroom, and bathroom each going off it. It didn't have much in the way of finishing touches and it could do with a lick of paint but he didn't like to bother Andy about that. He'd been good enough to not only take him in after he'd come out of prison but he'd given him a job too which was a real bonus, especially as Patricia had put her spoke in about it. David hadn't said much. He always acted like Wayne just wasn't there whenever he saw him. Wayne didn't blame him for that. He'd have probably done the same in his position.

He sat down but couldn't relax. He switched on the TV but he wasn't taking any notice of whatever was spouting out of the mouth of whatever talking head filled the screen. He put some music on but even his most favourite tunes were irritating him. What was it about the human condition that made everybody want to be with someone? People who said they didn't need anyone were such stupid liars. He picked up a cushion and held it tightly to him. Why does your life have to depend on the presence of just one of the millions who make up the human race? It had always been Wayne's trouble. He'd always needed someone. But he'd always wrecked it. He'd driven them all away. Except for his own mother who'd died when he was so young he could barely remember her. Then there was his father. He hadn't been there for him when he was sick because he'd been in prison. He'd attended his funeral on special release handcuffed to two prison officers and with everybody's eyes, especially Beryl's, stabbing him like the sharpest daggers. He'd grieved alone in his cell every night for weeks. He'd also grieved over the loss of every woman he'd ever had feelings for. Like Jill, Amanda, and, the greatest love of his life, Susan. Sweet, lovely Susan whose life he'd corroded with his poison.

He almost leapt out of his skin when the doorbell rang. He checked himself over in the mirror, He wiped his hands down his shirt and then, after the final hesitation, he opened the door. Stephanie stood there with a bottle of Australia's finest sparkling wines.

'This has been in my fridge all day' she said. 'But it's starting to get warm now so get a couple of glasses and let's do it some damage'.

'Sure thing' said Wayne, smiling. He took a couple of long glasses out of the cupboard in his tiny kitchen that was only really big enough for one person to be in at a time.

'I hope that wherever you're planning for us to eat tonight is within walking distance?' said Stephanie as Wayne poured the wine into the two glasses and handed one to Stephanie.

'Oh yeah' he answered. 'It's a little Italian place just a couple of minutes up the road'.

'How did you know I wanted pizza tonight?'

'I didn't'. He held up his glass. 'Shall we drink a toast?'

'Yes' said Stephanie. 'But I need to ask you something first'.

'What's that?'

'Wayne, when were you going to tell me about Susan and the time you spent in prison?'

Wayne suddenly lost his thirst. He placed the glass down and sat on the end of the sofa. This was like the day of reckoning. He knew it would come but he hadn't really prepared himself. Stephanie seemed like a fair minded person but still it felt like he was going on trial again.

'How did you find out?'

'That's not important'.

'Well you're working for Patricia so it doesn't take a rocket scientist'.

Stephanie had gone onto the internet after Patricia had told her about Wayne and she'd found plenty of coverage about the murder of Susan Hamilton who'd been found dead at the property of her husband, Wayne Hamilton, out at Dural on August 19, 1987. He'd made a confession to police and following the trial six months later he'd been sent down for twenty-five years. He'd refused the offer of parole three times but was finally released just over a couple of years ago after he'd served twenty-three out of his twenty-five year sentence.

'Why did you refuse parole, Wayne?'

'I didn't think I deserved it' Wayne answered. He was staring straight ahead into space. 'I didn't think I had the right to freedom after what I'd done. I didn't think I'd been in there long enough. And I saw prison as the only place where I could contain myself and purge all the badness out of me'.

'Tell me about Susan'.

'I was in love with her. I'd have done anything for her but I was a different man back then, Stephanie. What am I saying? I wasn't a man. I was a sad excuse for a man. All I wanted was somebody to make me feel good about myself. Nobody had ever done that. Not Patricia who I'm sure you know was my step-mother, and not even my father. He was another one who I loved with my life but who couldn't seem to bring himself to think the same about me. I spent years either trying to please him or destroy him. Then when I met Susan I actually caught a glimpse of the man I could be. I felt myself growing up in ways I'd never known before even though Patricia, Beryl, the Fiona Thompson who used to manage this place, and a woman called Caroline Morrell were all over our relationship trying to tear us apart. We got married and even during the ceremony her father David tried to stop it. Nobody wanted us to be happy because nobody wanted me to be happy. I was the real target. And I admit I'd done some pretty nasty stuff and I deserved all I got but so had all of them. They'd all stirred the pot at some time or another. Susan and I were happy for a brief time but then we had some problems and she had an affair with a guy called Glen. I was insane with jealousy and I mean I was getting way out there. I tried to force her to stay with me but then she faked her own suicide. Imagine that? The woman you love with all your heart is so desperate to get away from you that she pretends to be dead. But when I knew she'd faked it I had to try and get her back. She didn't want to come back. She came to the house one day and I lost it'.

'That's quite a story'.

'That's why I was terrified about telling you'.

'It sounds like you ran with a pretty scary crowd back then'.

'You don't know the half of it' said Wayne, softly. 'But I wasn't blameless, Stephanie. I became a very ugly person. I thought Susan could change me and bring out that side of me that I knew was there but kept getting buried in all the games and the lies and the manipulation. Growing up with Patricia I learnt from one of the best in the business. It would take me the rest of the week day and night to tell you all about what she's got up to over the years'.

Stephanie placed her hand on Wayne's back. 'Wayne, come and sit next to me properly'.

'You're going to tell me you're calling it all off?'

'No'

'Seriously?' Wayne questioned as he joined Stephanie on the sofa. 'You don't want to run away from me as fast as you can?'

'Wayne, I believe in giving people second chances' said Stephanie. 'I have met people who've committed murder before'.

'But have you actually gone out with one before?'

'No' said Stephanie. 'I have to admit that is a new one on me'.

'Then how come you're being so understanding? I don't deserve it'.

'You seem to make up your own mind a lot about what you deserve and what you don't. Can't you hand that judgment over to me for once?'

'I'm too bloody scared to'.

'Wayne you've served your time and I can understand why you didn't tell me about all this before. But I'm not one of those women who's possessive and needy and rings you up playing hell if you haven't answered my text message after five minutes. You and I are grown ups and I haven't led a blemish free life'.

'Have you murdered someone?'

'Well no but … '

' … well then you can't compare, Stephanie'.

'Wayne, this isn't about some kind of scorecard'.

'I know' said Wayne, feeling stupid. 'I'm not making a great job of this'.

'Wayne, just tell me what it is you need'.

'I need to make someone happy, Stephanie' said Wayne. 'And I need someone to love me and make me feel good about myself'.

'Will you settle for a bottle of sparkling wine and dinner to start with?' asked Stephanie who then linked her hand with Wayne's. 'I can help you put it all behind you but you have to trust me and you have to be honest with me. No secrets, no lies'.

'I'm not that person anymore'.

'Then don't ever give me reason to doubt that'.

Wayne looked at Stephanie and smiled. There were tears in his eyes. 'Ready for that toast?'

'I think so'.

Wayne handed Stephanie her glass and raised his own. 'Then allow me' he said. 'To an honest relationship'

'That does us both the world of good'.

The next morning Stephanie woke up and after a second or two she remembered she was in Wayne's bed. She lifted herself up on her elbows when he came in from the shower all wet with a blue towel wrapped round his waist. He looked so sexy with all the hair on his chest and stomach wet and sticking to his skin.

'Good morning, handsome' said Stephanie.

Wayne sat on the edge of the bed, leaned down and kissed her. 'Hi'.

'Why the long face?'

'I'm sorry about last night'.

'What are you sorry about?'

'I'm a little out of practice when it comes to sex'.

'You were a little eager' said Stephanie. 'But it didn't matter'.

'I was useless' said Wayne. 'It was all over way too quickly'.

Stephanie sat up and linked her hands round the back of his neck before kissing him. 'Well you really are living up to the honesty thing. Look Wayne, it happens to all men and some can't claim it's because they're out of practice'.

Wayne smiled. 'Where did you come from?'

Stephanie smiled back at him. 'I come from Nottingham in England. I told you that'.

'Do you fancy some breakfast?'

'Not yet' said Stephanie. She tugged at the towel Wayne had round his waist and loosened it. 'I want you to get back into bed because practice makes perfect and the more we practice the sooner we'll be perfect'.

'But I'm all wet'.

'Well I expect to be all wet too shortly' said Stephanie. 'In all the right places'.

'I think I've just died and gone to Heaven'.

Later that morning Stephanie persuaded Wayne to ask Andy for a day off and join her for her trip up to Palm Beach. He said he would and that he'd do the driving too.

'Did Andy mind you taking the day off?'

'No' said Wayne. 'I've never asked him before'.

'Never?'

'Never' Wayne confirmed. 'Just a few days ago I never would've thought I'd be doing this with you today'.

'And then I walked into your garden'.

'You most certainly did'.

'So we do have something to thank Patricia for' said Stephanie. 'I mean, if she hadn't have hired me then we may never have met'.

'Well that's the first time in the fifty years she's been in my life that she's ever done anything positive for me'.

'Is she really that bad?'

'Think of the worst human being you've ever met in your life and multiply them a thousand times'.

'Even when you were a child?'

'Well she was never big on showing maternal love' said Wayne. 'I think even her daughter Angela would say that'.

'Why wasn't her son John there too?'

'Well that goes back to the early sixties when she and David turned up at the house that's now Fiona Thompson House with the twins and Fiona took them in. A few days later Patricia walked out taking Angela with her and leaving John behind'.

'I can understand why she'd just want to walk away if they were in strife but why take Angela and not John?'

'Apparently she said that John reminded her of the twins' father who she hated'.

'But hang on, their father was David who I thought she'd loved all her life?'

'Oh she has. But there's always something hidden under whatever Patricia does. A year after John came back into her life, and that really is a long story for another time, it was John and Angela's twenty-first birthday party which David and Beryl held down in Melbourne. Patricia was told she wasn't invited because of a rift that had developed between her and Angela. Anyway, Patricia being Patricia she turned up, David wouldn't let her in and so she blurted out that he wasn't the twins' father and that she was pregnant when she met him'.

'Phew! Give me oxygen after all that'.

'Oh there's more. The twins' real father, a guy called Martin Healy who was in the air force, had been married at the time he had his affair with Patricia and she got pregnant. He wanted her to have an abortion and that's why she hated him. Anyway, John traced him and found he was a widower with three other kids. He started seeing Patricia again who by this time had left Gordon but wasn't yet back with David, and after a while he proposed to her. She agreed to marry him but it was only an act on her part. You see, she planned to stand Martin up at the altar for having tried to get her to have an abortion all those years ago. She's a big one for revenge is Patricia. When Martin found this out it was kind of the last straw'.

'He was having other problems?'

'Yes. He was a Group Captain with the air force and something had happened in his past which he never thought would come to light and which would cast a big black cloud over his record. But someone had found out and was about to expose him. Added to what Patricia was planning to do to him he snapped'.

'What did he do?'

'He shot himself'.

'Good God. And she got back together with David after that?'

'No, after that she fell in with a guy called Stephan Morrell but look, I really don't want to spend the day talking about Patricia'.

'No, I understand' said Stephanie. 'But David must love her very much?'

'Oh he does. He always has done. More fool him'.

When they got up to Palm Beach they couldn't fail to be impressed by the place on this hot, sunny day. Wayne hadn't been there since before he went inside and Stephanie had only been this far up the coast a handful of times since she'd been living in Australia. Wayne parked the car in one of the spaces where they got a clear view of the whole peninsula stretching out ahead of them. There was a gentle yet not unwelcome breeze coming off the ocean that was crashing into the rocks meters below at the bottom of the cliffs. In the other direction was the wooded area where Neil Jenkins' car had been found. And just beyond that was the cordoned off crime scene where the discovery of the body of the unknown woman was discovered.

'What do you think happened here?' asked Wayne after they'd got out of the car and paused to stretch their legs.

'I don't know' said Stephanie. 'But people don't just vanish. Neil Jenkins had a reason for running from his car that night and for dropping the life that he'd had until then'.

'It must've been a pretty devastating reason to make him walk out on everything and everyone he knew'

'Did you ever think about doing that when you were going through it?' Stephanie asked.

'I'll admit that it crossed my mind, yes' said Wayne. He ran his thumb across his chin.

'Did you ever think of doing anything even more drastic?'

'A couple of times' Wayne admitted. 'But I don't think I had the guts when it came to it. You don't think suicide was the case with Neil Jenkins?'

'I thought it might've been initially' said Stephanie. 'But I don't think so anymore'.

'But why did he drive all the way up here?' Wayne wondered. 'Why didn't he just take off from Fiona Thompson House?'

'Perhaps he was meeting someone?' Stephanie suggested.

'The woman in his car who ended up dead?'

'Well she's the safest bet at this stage' said Stephanie.

'Could it have something to do with money?'

'Well he didn't seem the gambling sort and Andy says there were no signs of any financial problems'.

'This really is a mystery, isn't it'.

'Well not for long I hope' said Stephanie. 'I need Patricia to pay me. I've been splashing out a bit lately including on a ticket home for Christmas'.

'What? You're going back to England for Christmas?'

'I'll only be gone a couple of weeks'.

'What? That's a lifetime'.

Stephanie smiled at the wounded child look Wayne was putting on. 'Take that daft look off your face'.

'You have your wicked way with me and then tell me you're shooting off to the other side of world for Christmas. I feel used'.

They looked at each other and laughed.

'It's good feeling like a kid again, isn't it' said Stephanie.

'Sure is'.

'Well we've got to be adults for a while now. We've got work to do. I mean, you didn't think I'd invited you along just so I can stare at your bum all day, did you?'

Neil Jenkins car had been found at the bend in an L-shaped lane that went through the wooded area from one main road to another. The trees made it a secluded spot even during the day so Stephanie thought that at night it must be quite spooky.

'Did the police check for footprints?' asked Wayne. 'It would seem like an obvious thing to do'.

'Apparently there was only one set and they fitted the size of a man's feet leading from the driver's side towards the cliffs. But they couldn't find any further prints beyond the grass that he would've had to cross if he had intended to throw himself off'.

'So he changed direction'.

'Looks that way' said Stephanie. 'But why do you think he did that?'

'He could've been distracted by the woman in his car?'

'She was trying to stop him from jumping over the cliff? If that was correct then why weren't any of her footprints found in the same place? The police didn't check on the other side of the car'.

'You're joking?'

'I'm not. It was an oversight at the very least'.

'They'd made up their minds more or less straight away and then made whatever evidence they could find fit their theory of suicide'.

'It wouldn't be the first time they've done that' said Stephanie. 'And at the time it would make sense because they had no idea of a dead woman being part of the mix. They only found the woman's DNA in the car after they'd taken it in for examination'.

'And now the body of a woman who'd been in Neil's car makes them and their original theories look a little stupid'.

'Yes, to say the least' said Stephanie. 'So now they'll try and make out like Neil Jenkins murdered the woman and to support their assertions they'll ask why Neil Jenkins didn't stick around. I have to find out who that woman was and what she meant to Neil Jenkins, Wayne. Otherwise I might start thinking that he killed her myself'.

FIONA THOMPSON FIVE

Stephanie was on her way to see Neil Jenkins mother. As she drove out to the house she was contemplating her emerging relationship with Wayne. Not that she was having second thoughts but finding out that he'd murdered his wife was a little distracting in some ways. She had to believe him when he said that he wasn't anything like the man he'd been back then and she did believe him. His soul had been damaged. If she was a psychiatrist and had him on her couch she'd probably conclude that he'd never got over the loss of his mother at such a young age and that his father Gordon may have spent his life blaming Wayne for his wife's death it in some way and that's why he'd put so much distance between himself and his son. Then with Patricia for a step-mother and all the other characters who'd populated his life back then the poor bugger never would've stood a bloody chance.

Connie Weston lived out at St. Mary's which was about thirty miles west of the centre of Sydney. It was a fairly solidly white blue collar sort of area with cricket played on the green and flowers blooming like lines of regimented soldiers along the borders of each well kept garden. Stephanie thought she'd die in a place like this where everybody knew everybody else's business and nobody was allowed to deviate from the path of having kids whether you wanted them or not. You couldn't do anything different or stretch your horizons. You had to do what was expected or else you were labeled as someone who thought they were above themselves. And if anything went wrong in your boring as hell narrowly defined life then you could always blame it on all those who were lower down on the social scale from you or, better still, you could always use the common default position of white working class people and blame it on the immigrants when you're dismissed from your job because you're too lazy, too complacent or too fucking incompetent. Stephanie couldn't see one face that wasn't white and it reminded her of the area of Nottingham back in England where she grew up.

When she was little it was all white like this but then immigrants, beginning with Asians who were kicked out of their homes by Idi Amin in Uganda, started moving in and that's when salt of the earth types like her parents turned into out and out racists. Stephanie never understood why. What difference did the colour of someone's skin make? To her racism just didn't make sense. If you had a problem with someone then it was because of the kind of person they were, not because of their race or creed. She had regular fights with her parents over it especially when she made friends with some of what her father called 'the Paki tribe'. Her father had the gall to call himself a Christian because he went to church every Sunday morning but he didn't act like one the rest of the week with his regularly stated absolute condemnation of 'all these brown skins coming in from everywhere and stinking the place out with their curries'. She'd never really got on with her father. She wondered what he'd make of Wayne. If he was brown or black her father wouldn't have given him a chance under any circumstances. But he was white so that would let him off having a criminal record.

She parked outside the weatherboard bungalow where Connie Weston lived. It was characteristic of all the properties in the area and painted in a kind of off white and there were tall bushes going up and down the sides. She stepped onto the porch at the front and knocked on the front door. When Connie answered she looked suspicious and Stephanie explained why she was there.

'Why do you want to find Neil?' asked Connie.

'A friend of his has hired me because she's worried about what happened to him' said Stephanie who looked Connie up and down fleetingly. She was in a pair of cotton type white trousers and a shiny blue silk looking blouse. It made her look older than Patricia Palmer and yet she was probably a good ten years younger than her.

'She? Was it that Patricia woman? Patricia Palmer?'

'Yes, that's right' said Stephanie. Think of the devil and her name is mentioned, thought Stephanie. 'Do you know her?'

'She's been here a couple of times' groaned Connie. 'I had to ask her to leave the last time'.

'Why was that?'

'She threw a mental at me. Told me I was an inadequate mother and that no wonder my son hated me. Well I don't expect any of my kids to hate me. I expect them to respect me because I'm the mother'.

Oh no, thought Stephanie, respect has to be earned and she'd always considered it such an uneducated and ignorant view of parents to believe their children's respect should be automatic. She didn't think her own sons James and Matthew respected her and she wouldn't blame them if they didn't. After all, she'd let them leave Australia and go back to England without her. She had no right to their respect and had to do all she could to earn it.

'Patricia Palmer wanted answers that I couldn't give her and I felt a bit threatened by the way she was acting up' Connie went on. 'She was shouting and really losing it. Her husband seemed like quite a decent bloke and he had to tell her to calm down. I was bloody glad to see the back of her, I can tell you'.

Interesting, thought Stephanie. Why would Patricia get so upset? Even if she did miss her friend and was desperate to know what had happened to him, why would she have reason to make Connie Weston feel so threatened?

'Well Connie, could I come in so we can talk? I promise I won't lose my rag'.

'Well, okay' said Connie, leading her inside. 'But I'm getting rather tired of this. The police were here yesterday trying to link Neil with the murder of that woman they found'.

'You don't think he had anything to do with that?'

'My son may have been a lot of things but he wasn't a murderer'.

'How do you mean by a lot of things?'

'He was one of those homosexuals'.

'From what I can gather it wasn't quite as simple as that'.

'He slept with other men. How much more simple could it get?'

'Well the last time I looked that wasn't against the law'.

'Well I don't hold with that kind of thing' Connie asserted. 'It may not be a very modern way of looking at it but both my husband Dennis and I think that it isn't natural and is a perversion. There, I've said it'.

'So is marrying a man who won't accept your son because he's mixed race'.

'How dare you talk to me like that!'

'Does the truth hurt, Connie? Well clearly it does but you know what? Nobody I've spoken to has had a bad word to say about your son. They all say he was charming, funny, a good and loyal friend. You should be proud of him but instead you bad mouth him to me'.

'Well it wasn't as cut and dried as you say'.

'Perhaps it wasn't but did you or did you not leave Neil with your mother because your husband Dennis wouldn't accept him because he was mixed race?' She watched as Connie's face showed complete capitulation. 'You owe him, Connie. You owe him because everybody loved him except you, his mother'.

Connie made them both a coffee and they sat at her kitchen table. Stephanie looked round and could see that the place needed a bit of doing up. Paint and wallpaper were both peeling in some places and the kitchen looked long overdue for a makeover.

'Neil always said that he felt alienated from his own life' said Connie. 'I never understood what he meant'.

'Did you try?'

'Not really, no. He was always whining about something and I had two other children to bring up'.

'Who were both white'.

'Well of course they were white' Connie retorted. 'Their father and I are both white so it stands to reason'.

'But Neil wasn't white because his father wasn't. And that was the problem wasn't it'.

'I was very much in love with Neil's father' said Connie, quietly. 'I hadn't been working at St. Vincent's hospital for very long when I met Yosef. I had precious little in the way of qualifications and I had a very lowly kind of administration job in his department but he was this tall very dashing very handsome man from the other side of the world who noticed me and made me feel very special. What girl wouldn't fall for all that? But really what happened was that a married man took advantage of a naïve young Aussie girl from the suburbs'.

'That's how you see it?'

'Well is there another way to see it?'

'Well, if I can be so bold, how quickly did you become involved with him?'

'You mean how soon was it before I slept with him? Well I'll tell you it was six months and during that time he came and met my parents, took my two younger brothers out on visits here, there, and everywhere. He had this big car and lots of money but he was also very generous and very kind'.

'So if you were going out for six months before anything physical happened then is it really truthful to say that he took advantage of you?'

'Is this what you call investigation?' asked Connie, sharply. 'Because all you're doing is putting me in the dock'.

'Connie, if I'm going to find your son then I need a true and complete picture of his entire life so I can decide where to concentrate my efforts. And that sometimes means I have to be a little forthright'.

'You're only interested because Patricia Palmer is paying you so don't jump on your high horse and try and make out like you're under some moral obligation to find a missing person because I won't believe it'.

'I didn't say that' said Stephanie, firmly. 'And if you think that I did then you've read me all wrong, Connie. Look, apart from the fact that I'm being paid I'm also curious to know why a young man like Neil would run away in such dramatic circumstances. And as his mother I assumed you'd want to know too'.

'Look, Neil was trouble to me since the day he was born, in fact, it started before then' said Connie, remembering days way back when she thought her future had been snatched away from her. 'I should've had him adopted but my mother wouldn't hear of it'.

'Why not?'

'Because my mother was a very needy person' Connie answered. 'She needed to have people around her to care for. She needed to have people dependent on her and I'm one of six so when we were growing up and showing signs of flying the nest she latched on to a grandchild like a heat seeking missile, particularly in the circumstances that Neil was coming into the world. It meant that she could carry on being needed and that was more important to her than my needs or the needs of my child. The baby basically became hers and I didn't really have much of a say. She said she'd love the baby and that's all it would need. My mother meant well but she wasn't the smartest and she didn't think about what it would be like for the child to be brought up in an area like this'.

'What did you mean?'

'Well look around you, love. A mixed race child was always going to stick out round here like a bloody shag on a rock. Neil was bullied at school because he looked different'.

'And what did you do about that?'

'What did I do?'

'Well as his mother?'

'Look, he didn't live with me by then so it wasn't my problem. I left it to my mother to try and sort out but what could she do? She couldn't get him a skin transplant. He was doomed from the word go. My mother was so convinced that everything would have a fairy tale ending because she loved Neil unconditionally'.

'Wasn't that your job as his mother?'

'There you go again with your sticks and stones. Let me ask, do you have any children?'

'Yes, I have two sons'.

Connie looked surprised. 'Oh. I see. I thought you were one of them do-gooders who think they know all about being a parent when they've never had a kid'.

Stephanie decided not to explain her situation with James and Matthew and the fact that they'd been on the opposite side of the world from her for most of their lives. She didn't want to be too hard on Connie but she did seem to have screwed up Neil's life in a big way. Of course Connie would never admit that. She was the sort who always had to find someone or something else to blame.

'Then there was a problem when he went to school. My mother had school report after school report telling her how bloody clever Neil was and that he should be thinking about going on to university. But we're not the sort of family who become teachers or doctors or lawyers. We're trades people. University was never on the cards because my mother couldn't afford to support him through it and we certainly weren't going to even though we probably could've done'.

'So you could've supported your son through university but you didn't because you didn't believe that people from your kind of family did anything with their lives?'

'That's about the size of it, yes'.

'Unbelievable'.

'Look, I've told you before that if all you've come here to do is to pick holes in my mothering skills then you can just get lost, lady'.

'I need to find your son'.

'Yeah, so you can get your paycheck' scoffed Connie. 'Well I told his father where to get off and you can take a single ticket to the same bloody place!'

'His father?'

'Get out'.

'When did you speak to his father?'

Connie couldn't believe how stupid she'd been to blurt out a reference to Neil's father. Everything should just be left well alone. Now it could only mean trouble.

'Yosef came back from the Middle East when Neil was nine years old. I'd been married just over a year then and I was living here with Dennis. Neil was living half an hour away with my mother. Yosef wanted to see him. He said he wanted to connect with his son whatever that means. He said he wanted to try and make it up to him, try and give him something back for all the lost years'.

'So what happened?'

'I told Yosef to take a running jump'.

'You didn't tell Neil that his father wanted to see him?'

'Not until the row we had a week before he disappeared, no'.

'You denied him that chance'.

'Why are you looking at me like that?'

'Well I'm trying to imagine it from Neil's perspective. You stopped him having a relationship with his father'.

'I had every right to'.

'No you didn't, Connie'.

'Yosef had hurt me! I didn't know he was married or else I'd never have slept with him'.

'So you used Neil to get back at his father and yet Neil wasn't even living with you so what skin would it have been off your nose?'

'I had the power to prevent it and so I did'.

'With no thought for the consequences down the years? How did Neil react to that bombshell?'

'He wasn't happy'.

'I should think not'.

'But he had his own bombshell to drop'.

Stephanie paused. 'And are you going to tell me what that was?'

'His sister, or his half-sister, had tracked him down. Her name was Mariam. Yosef had died about six months earlier but before he did he'd told her all about Neil. She wanted to get to know her brother and she was the one who told him I'd sent his father packing all those years ago. He said he'd never forgive me. That was the last time I saw him'.

'Connie, do you miss your son?'

Connie thought for a moment and then said 'No' she said. 'I'd like to say that I do but no, I don't. I think about him from time to time and I suppose I hope he's alright. But you see, after my mother died and Neil went to live at Fiona Thompson House I saw that as the end. I no longer had to see him because he was living with my mother. What he did after that was really up to him and nothing to do with me'.

On the drive back into the city Stephanie started putting some more of the pieces together. Connie had given her Mariam's full name which gave Stephanie a potentially very positive lead on finding out what happened to Neil. She was certain it had been Mariam who was the mystery person Neil had been seeing in the weeks before he disappeared. She was also certain that Mariam must've been the woman who'd been found dead near Neil's car. But surely Neil would have no motive to kill her? The police report said that she'd been shot. Could Neil have been capable of that and then spent these past three years as nothing more than a fugitive?

She pulled up outside a row of half a dozen shops and got herself a takeaway coffee. She decided to sit and drink it before driving on and whilst she did so she called Maddy Green.

'I think I may be able to identify the mystery dead woman' she announced to Maddy's obvious interest. It was always good for a constable to deliver a major lead in a murder investigation. It got you noticed. 'I think her name is Mariam al-Ashwari. She's the daughter of Dr. Yosef al-Ashwari who was opthalmics registrar at St. Vincent's in the mid 1980's'.

'And the father of Neil Jenkins' said Maddy.

'Precisely' said Stephanie. 'Mariam made contact with Neil after their father's death'.

'And Neil decided to keep her secret'.

'Well he may have wanted to get to know her first' Stephanie suggested. 'She was his first contact with his father's family'.

'I agree that's understandable' said Maddy. 'How did you find this out anyway?'

'Neil's mother'.

'But we interviewed her and she said nothing about Mariam?'

'Maybe I made some kind of deeper connection, I don't know' said Stephanie. 'But tell me, didn't the police look into anything to do with Neil's father as part of their investigation into his disappearance?'

Maddy paused. 'No' she said. She cleared her throat. 'We didn't'.

'But surely that would've been an obvious part of Neil's life to look into?'

'You'd have thought so' said Maddy. 'I can't say anymore because I don't know I'm afraid. Yes, we should've but we didn't and I don't know why. Sorry'.

The next morning Stephanie woke up with Wayne's arms wrapped tenderly around her.

'Hi' she whispered.

'Hi'.

'What time is it?'

'It's almost seven' said Wayne. 'Are you okay?'

'Yeah? Why?'

'You were crying in the middle of the night' said Wayne. 'I reached out to hold you and you cried on my shoulder'.

'I'm sorry'.

'No need to be sorry' said Wayne. 'Do you want to talk about it?'

It had been some time since Stephanie had had a man to confide in. 'It's my boys'.

'They're back in England, right?'

'Yes. They haven't lived with me since they were six years old. James is now eighteen and Matthew is sixteen. I think about them all the time but this case has really made me reflect on the past as far as they're concerned and I don't come out of it very well. I'm their mother. I should've been there all the time. All those years have been lost. You can't get them back'.

'I understand. Like I want to understand everything about you'.

Stephanie ran her fingers up and down Wayne's fury arms. 'You're doing a great job, believe me'.

'I've got a son out there somewhere'.

'You have?'

'I was fifteen and I got a little too friendly with one of the local girls. Patricia paid the family off to avoid a scandal affecting our family'.

'She's always there, isn't she?'

'Patricia? Oh yes. The girl had a little boy who she called Tick. He ended up in the foster care system but he came back into my life when I was going through everything with Susan and to be honest he was a God send. I was planning to keep him but there was a misunderstanding over something and he hid in the boot of Susan's car which I sent to be crushed as part of my way of forgetting all about Susan, not knowing that Tick was hiding in the boot. I managed to find him just in time but the social services people, with the help of Patricia who had it in for me at the time, sent him straight back to his foster parents and I haven't seen or heard from him since'.

'Oh Wayne' said Stephanie. 'I'm sorry'.

'Well I wouldn't try and find him now' said Wayne.

'Why wouldn't you?'

'It's too late and he's probably too established in whatever life he has for me to come along and rumble everything. Besides, I've got nothing to offer him'.

'You've got yourself, Wayne, and the fact that you're his father'.

'But I've only been in his life for a few brief moments'.

'Which I've no doubt he'll remember'.

Wayne kissed the top of Stephanie's head. 'Well in the meantime you my dear Stephanie can still save the day with your sons'.

'Well I'm hoping'.

Wayne got out of bed and put on a pair of briefs before coming over to Stephanie's side and kissing her. 'Why don't you call them? I'm going to make some raisin toast and tea for breakfast. Call them whilst I'm getting all that done. Go on'.

Stephanie smiled as she watched Wayne put on his bathrobe. He really was a big old sensitive soul.

'Yes, boss' said Stephanie. 'But on one condition'.

'What's that?'

'That you do agree to let me help you find Tick?'

'I'll think about it. Now make that call'.

Stephanie dialed one of the two numbers she had programmed into her mobile for her two sons. It still amazed her one small piece of metal and plastic in her hand could make a connection with someone on the other side of the world who was holding something similar. She was more than familiar with the time change. If it was seven o'clock here in Sydney then it was about ten o'clock last night back in the UK.

'Mum?'

'James? Yes, it's me darling. How are you?'

'I'm good thanks, Mum. So you're coming over for Christmas? Awesome'.

'Yes' said Stephanie nervously. 'Will you and Matthew be around?'

'You bet' said James. 'Your planned visit has caused quite a stir in all the right ways, Mum. Gran has got it all organized. Matthew and I are coming over to her place for dinner with you on Christmas Eve'.

'Really?' said Stephanie who felt like bursting into tears. 'That's fantastic news'.

'And then we're getting together with all your side of the family for a buffet lunch at Uncle Colin's on Boxing Day'.

Stephanie couldn't get over how it was all coming together for her Christmas return to England. She felt an overwhelming sense of joy even now just talking to James on the phone.

'Are you still there, Mum?'

'Yes' said Stephanie, holding back the tears. 'I'm just excited at all these Christmas arrangements'.

'We are too, Mum. But look, it'll be great to see Gran and all the family but could we have lunch or dinner or something just the three of us sometime whilst you're here? Matthew and I would just like you to ourselves for a while, you know?'

Stephanie bit her lip. 'I do know and yes, we will do that. But I'm out of touch with the restaurants in Nottingham so you'll have to come up with a place for us to go'.

'No problem, I'll be on to it' said James. 'And Mum?'

'Yes, darling?'

'It will be great to see you'.

'Well it looks like everything is in order, Andy' said Patricia. She'd been having her monthly accounts meeting with Andy in his flat at Fiona Thompson House. The meeting covered all seven of the properties that Andy managed for Patricia.

'Isn't it always?'

'Yes, but I wouldn't want you getting complacent'.

Andy had to smile. He'd been doing this for Patricia now for twenty years and still she had to slip in the odd barbed comment. 'Of course not'.

'Now that we've finished with the accounts, Andy, I want to ask you to do something else for me'.

'Oh?'

'I want you to keep an eye on Wayne and his relationship with Stephanie Marshall'.

'You want me to spy on them?'

'Well that's not quite how I'd put it'.

'But it amounts to the same thing'.

'Andy, I've employed Stephanie to find a very dear friend of both of us and Wayne has hated me all his life'.

'Patricia, he's really past all that now' said Andy.

'Andy, a leopard doesn't change its spots like that'.

'It wasn't like that, Patricia. It was over twenty years in prison. It changed him for the better and you'd see that for yourself if you condescended to actually speak to him instead of ignoring him all the time'.

'Andy, my loyalties are with David and Wayne murdered his daughter. Or have you forgotten that little detail?'

'Susan was no angel, Patricia. We both know that'.

'But she didn't deserve to die like that, Andy'.

'I agree but Wayne has done his time'

'As far as the state is concerned, yes. But that doesn't always transfer into people's emotions'.

'Patricia, just look at the facts. There's Beryl, Wayne's step-mother and widow of his father, and Robert, Wayne's step-brother, both millionaires down there in Melbourne from the success of Air Australia, an airline which developed from Sanders' Air Charter which Wayne financed in the early days to avoid his father Gordon going bankrupt. Nobody would deny that he's entitled to a cut of that very large cake but has he gone after it? No. Patricia, he hasn't got two cents to rub together and yet he's not even prepared to fight for what's rightfully his because he doesn't want to be drawn back into those old dark days. That should tell you what a changed person he is'.

'Sorry Andy, but I'll never trust him. I admire you for sticking by him but don't expect me to. He tried to ruin me on more than one occasion'.

'Oh and of course you did nothing to provoke that kind of revenge action, did you? Don't try and pull the wool over my eyes, Patricia. I was there, remember? I witnessed a lot of the tricks you pulled'.

'Yes, well that's the trouble with people like me. Nobody believes me when I am being honest'.

'Well if you're not prepared to give Wayne the benefit of the doubt then why should anyone grant it to you?'

'Because in your case I'm your employer and you need to remember that'.

'Oh I do' answered Andy, testily. 'But please don't go meddling in Wayne's life because of some old grudge. He's happier now than I think I've ever seen him'.

'Andy, I don't think you get how much trouble I could be in. I could end up losing everything, including this place. I would not be doing myself any favours if I didn't keep an eye on someone who was once my mortal enemy and who's now living in my building'.

'Was once your mortal enemy, Patricia. He isn't anymore'.

'Yes, well we'll wait and see, Andy. We'll wait and see'.

Even though David Palmer was Robert's natural father, Robert had always considered his step-father Gordon Hamilton to be his actual father. After all it was Gordon who'd brought him up and been there for him. During his childhood he'd only had periodical contact with

David but when Gordon a few years ago Robert felt like he should perhaps get to know David better. It hadn't started well. David had tried too hard and Robert hadn't been able to stop himself from being antagonistic over David's absence from his life. But over time a bridge had been built and now they'd certainly call themselves mates. It didn't include Patricia though. Robert wouldn't trust her as far as he could spit.

'Over here, Robert!' called David from the table when he saw Robert come through the door. They were meeting at their usual steak house in the Rocks area of Sydney. David had arrived there first and was already downing a beer. 'What do you want to drink, mate?'

'Ah, just a sparkling mineral water, David, thanks' said Robert who sat down and placed his briefcase beside him. He put his mobile phone and his tablet computer on the table. 'I've got meetings stacked all through this afternoon'.

'You've got time to have lunch with your old Dad, though?' said David, looking at his son with all the gadgets that told the world that he was a modern business executive. And he wasn't wearing a tie either. None of these successful businessmen today seemed to.

'Oh yes' said Robert. 'I made time for that, David'.

'When are you going back to Melbourne?'

'Tonight. I've asked them to reserve a seat for me on the half past eight departure'.

'The pleasures of being the boss eh?'

Robert was chief executive and major shareholder in Air Australia which now had the second biggest market share of domestic air travel in Australia flying a fleet of Airbus aircraft between all the major cities and taking all their bookings online. Passengers had to pay to check-in a suitcase and for all drinks and snacks onboard. It was run along the lines of the same business model pioneered by other so-called 'low cost' airlines in Europe and America. Robert owed his place at the helm to his step-father Gordon Hamilton who'd invested in the business started as Sanders Air Charter by the other major shareholder, Bill Sanders, who was now operations manager. The third shareholder was Beryl Hamilton.

'It keeps them on their toes'.

'So have Bill Sanders and your mother made it official?'

'Yeah, they have really' said Robert. 'I told Mum it was a bit silly them keeping it all hush, hush. They've known each other so long and know each other so well that it didn't take a massive leap to go from that to a romantic situation. And you can always tell when two people are a couple but trying to pretend not to be so people were asking, you know'.

'Well as long as she's happy'.

'Yes, she is, David. She is happy'.

Both David and Robert ordered medium rare steaks with side salad and jacket potatoes. David ordered another beer and Robert allowed himself a glass of red wine to have with his food.

'And what about you and Melissa?' David asked.

'What about us?'

'Well are you going to give me an excuse to buy a new suit anytime soon?'

'We're engaged'.

'Yes, and?'

'Well we live together'.

'And is that how you're going to leave it?'

'Ah look, I don't know, David. We're happy as we are'.

'And would she agree with that?'

'Why am I getting the third degree on my love life, David?'

'You're not. I'm just interested'.

'Kevin and Lynn have already made you a grandfather so you can't be waiting for that' said Robert. 'And their little Davey could be making you a great grandfather soon. I always laugh at the name little Davey. All four and a half meters of him and a rugby player to boot'.

David smiled at the thought of his grandson. 'Yeah. Little Davey has stuck since he was born. But look, Melissa is a really nice girl, Robert. I can't see you doing any better'.

Robert's patience was being sorely tested by David's line of questioning. 'And is that what you thought when you were married to my mother but secretly still in love with Patricia? Or when you shacked up with Patricia's sister Margaret?'

'Alright' said David, sucking it all up with a deep breath. 'I suppose I deserved that'.

'Look, David, I get that you were always in love with Patricia and that what you felt for my Mum was different, I get that, David, I'm a big boy and I get that. Both you and Mum came through it and have been happy since then and I'm pleased about that but David, I'm not you and I'm not Mum and I'm not Patricia or Gordon. I love Melissa but I'm just not sure if she's the one. You know what I'm saying, David?'

'I think I do, son' said David. 'You don't want to repeat the same mistakes that we all made'.

'That's it, yes. And I don't want to take that next step unless or until I am sure'.

They took a few moments to enjoy their food but there was a question burning inside David's head that he couldn't hold back on any longer.

'So, mate?' said David after he'd digested another mouthful of his steak. The meat was really good and tender. He rested his knife and fork on his plate. There was still some meat and some potato left for him to devour. 'Did you find anything out like I asked you to?'

'Yes, David' said Robert. 'I did some digging on who might have it in for poor innocent Patricia'.

'Yes, Robert, I get that you're not her biggest fan but that's not what or why I asked you'.

'Okay' said Robert. 'I'll put you out of your misery. David, the problems stem from the fact that Patricia's company, Palmer Holdings, took out three loans from a bank in Singapore to expand the business but she didn't declare those loans to the tax authorities here in Australia. Now it may not be her fault. She could've been badly advised financially. But the fact remains that she didn't pay her dues. Now as to the matter of who dobbed her, I haven't been able to get that far. But somebody did, David and they weren't doing it because they like Patricia'.

FIONA THOMPSON SEVEN

The main city branch of Southern Cross bank was at the far end of Elizabeth Street just a stone's throw from the harbour front. Stephanie knew the area well. She used to go regularly to an Indian restaurant near here that was one of the best she'd ever been to. Then it closed down all of a sudden. She never did find out why.

She introduced herself at the customer service desk and was taken through to a side office to meet the human resources manager who was called Alan Ford. He was a rather hefty looking guy in his early fifties and a little eccentric in his style of attire. He was wearing one of those thick looking soft cotton shirts with a green and blue crossover stripe pattern on it and a large tweed bow tie. A pair of dark grey trousers and a burgundy coloured wool waistcoat completed the look. He must be hot in all that she thought. His grey hair was thinning and he wore his thick rimmed glasses on the end of his nose.

'I know what you're thinking' he announced as he sat down. He had a slightly camp voice but Stephanie didn't like to make the automatic connection between being camp and being gay. She'd met many a camp straight man in her time.

'You do?'

'You were expecting a bright young thing'.

'Not really'.

'Well most of the HR jobs are taken by a much younger crowd than me these days. I'm one of those survivors whose managed to slip under the radar of the industrial fashion police'.

Stephanie inwardly sighed. She had a feeling that Alan Ford was going to be charming but bloody hard work.

'Why don't you tell me about Neil Jenkins? Did you know him?'

'Know him? He and I were very close' said Alan. 'There are many people working here at the bank as you can see and some you get on with and some you don't. But Neil and I were great mates. Oh everyone thinks I'm gay because I'm a little flamboyant but I'm not so there was nothing going on between us of a sexual nature. But he did confide in me about one thing. Mariam al-Ashwari was his half-sister and she'd come to Australia to make contact with him'.

'I thought so' said Stephanie. 'It makes sense'.

'I've been on to the police this morning because I met her on a couple of occasions'.

'Well you were honoured'.

'Yes, it seems so' Alan agreed. 'She was an absolutely charming young woman. And she was beautiful with shiny black hair and light brown skin. She was like you if I may say so in that she didn't need to wear a lot of make-up in to turn men's heads'.

Stephanie smiled self-consciously. 'You're a charmer, Alan'.

'Well I mean it. Anyway, she was a doctor and she lived in Zurich, Switzerland. Neil's father's family had fallen foul of the Assad regime in Damascus long before the current awful problems. They'd managed to get out and the family settled in Switzerland'.

'What kind of doctor was Mariam?'

'She was in ophthalmics like her father' Alan revealed. 'She and Neil hit it off straight away after she'd made contact with him and developed a close relationship over those few short weeks. It was still tough for him though. After all, they shared a father but Mariam and her brother had been part of his family. They'd had everything whilst Neil had been forced to settle for nothing. He knew it wasn't their fault and he didn't blame them but it still hurt'.

'Did Neil talk to Mariam about it?'

'Yes and she understood' said Alan. 'She was a very bright, intelligent woman and she understood perfectly why he would feel that. That's one of the reasons why she wanted to make it up to him'.

'In what way?'

'She'd come with permission from her mother to make Neil an offer for a share of his father's estate. It was a considerable offer amounting to half a million dollars. Neil was delighted, of course he was, because it opened up his choices in life and finally gave him something of what he felt he'd always deserved. But the money was secondary. It was the relationship he was developing with Mariam that mattered so much to him and what was making him so very happy. He couldn't believe that she'd crossed the world to acknowledge him on behalf of her father, their father. That was priceless to Neil. It was absolutely priceless to him'.

'So he wouldn't have killed her?'

'I made it clear in my statement to the police that the suggestion was ludicrous. The idea … the very idea that Neil could kill anyone especially someone he'd come to think the world of … well like I said before it is ludicrous'.

'So who did kill her? What do you think happened that night?'

'I've gone over and over it in my head a hundred times and I've even been up to Palm Beach myself to check the whole thing out but I'm as baffled as anybody'.

'Gut feeling?'

'That he may have witnessed something so traumatic that he ran and he hasn't been able to find his way back'.

'Traumatic as in witnessing the murder of his sister?'

'Yes' said Alan. 'I think they were going up to Palm Beach for a couple of days, after all it was the weekend when it happened, and they were ambushed in some way by robbers or criminals of some kind. Maybe he was taken and is yet to be found although the thought of that sends shivers down my spine. But one thing I am certain of. He didn't kill anyone, least of all Mariam'.

'Do you know if Neil accepted his sister's offer of a settlement from his father's estate?'

'Yes, he did' said Alan.

'He could fill a lot of emotional gaps with that. Had he received the money before he disappeared?'

'Yes and that's another thing the police are making something out of. They see it as another part of the motive he had for killing Mariam'.

'Well just how are they doing that?'

'Look, Stephanie, I like you and that's why I'm going to tell you something I think you should know, something that worried me a great deal before he disappeared and still does. For about two months some large sums of money were passing through Neil's bank account'.

'What do you mean by large?'

'Twenty grand each time and it happened on six occasions. The strange thing was though that the money was never in there for more than a couple of days'.

'But where did it come from and where did it go to?'

'I did some investigating of my own' said Alan. 'It came from Patricia Palmer'.

Stephanie sucked in air through her teeth. 'Patricia'.

'But I went further back. I managed to trace a line back to an account held by the Ramberg corporation. In case you didn't know they're one of Australia's biggest construction firms and Patricia has been on the board for many years'.

'And what happened to the money after it had been in Neil's account?'

'It went into an account owned by a company called Silky Secrets'.

Stephanie almost laughed. 'Silky secrets? Who the hell are they?'

'They're based down in Melbourne and they specialize in lingerie for the more naughty of ladies shall we say. They also do a line in sex toys and creams to aid the natural processes'.

'But why would Patricia be behind that?'

'I don't know'.

'But she was making it look like Neil was buying a hell of a lot of lingerie. Did Neil know about it?'

'I don't think he did, no, at least not initially'.

'So when did he find out?'

'Well the last tranche of money was much larger than the previous ones and that's when he did notice. It was a hundred thousand Australian dollars and soon after that his friendship with Patricia was broken and Neil kept the money. Patricia was furious. God, I've never seen someone so livid. Then on the day he disappeared he transferred the hundred thousand, along with the five hundred thousand settlement from his father, to an account at the Mallacca bank in Singapore'.

Stephanie thanked her lucky stars. Of all the banks in Singapore it could've gone to it went to the one where she had a pretty reliable contact.

'Now it makes it sound like he was planning to leave the country'.

'I know but he didn't mention anything. He never even hinted. He didn't give his notice in at the bank or anything. It's just something else about all this that is so mysterious'.

'Like so much else. Alan, did you tell the police at the time that you'd met Neil's sister?'

'Oh yes. But they didn't seem to think it was that important'.

'And did you tell them about this money that was going through Neil's account?'

Alan looked rather sheepish. 'No. I know I should've done but I was a little scared. Not only for myself but also I didn't want to drop Neil in it'.

'But how could he have been unaware of that kind of money going through his account?'

'Well he wasn't always good at checking his balances' Alan revealed. 'We went out for dinner once and it was his turn to pay. He handed over his card but it was declined because he hadn't checked his balance and he didn't have enough to pay for the meal. I paid it and it didn't matter at all but it was indicative of how he could be a little careless with his finances. Not to any great degree. He was just a bit lazy when it came to keeping up with things'.

'And he had no direct link with Ramberg?'

'No' Alan confirmed. 'His only connection was his friendship with Patricia who, like I said before has been a director of the company for many years'.

Stephanie went back to her office reeling with all the information Alan Ford had given to her about Neil Jenkins' financial affairs and also about his sister Mariam. She called Maddy Green who confirmed that Mariam al-Ashwari had never been on the missing persons list and nobody had made enquiries about her to the New South Wales police. But surely the hospital in Zurich where Mariam had worked would've tried to find out what had happened to her? And more importantly, her family, her sister and mother would've wanted to know?

Then there was the matter of the money being passed through his account.

Her thoughts were interrupted by the arrival of David Palmer.

'I'm sorry, I didn't make an appointment' said David.

'Oh don't worry about that' said Stephanie. 'I'm very pleased to meet you'.

'Yeah, well Pat doesn't know I'm here'.

'I see' said Stephanie, wondering why that would be. 'Do you want to tell me why?'

'Someone has dobbed Pat in to the tax authorities' David explained after he'd sat down. 'She's worried sick about it. She thinks she's going to lose everything if she's not careful'.

'Is she guilty?'

'She says not and I believe her. But the whole thing goes back to just over three years ago when she took out the first in a series of business loans from a bank in Singapore … '

Three years ago, thought Stephanie. About the same time Patricia was pushing money through Neil Jenkins' bank account. She decided she wasn't going to tell David anything about what she'd found out about Patricia and the trail of Ramberg money. She wanted to face Patricia with that herself.

' .. the tax office here is claiming she never paid her rightful dues to Canberra on those loans. She insists she left all that to her accountant but the odd thing is that he's nowhere to be found. Stephanie, I know you're looking for Neil Jenkins on behalf of Pat at the moment but could you see if you have any time to get to the bottom of this other matter? I'll pay you separately and, like I said, I want it kept confidential between you and me'.

'Discretion is the soul of my business, David'.

'I know but I just wanted to make sure. Oh and don't worry about your fee because I've got more than enough to cover that and whatever you end up charging Pat if the worst comes to the worst'.

'Will it stretch to a short trip to Singapore?'

'I don't see why not' said David. 'If it means you getting a result'.

'Good' said Stephanie. 'Because I think I might find some useful information out if I go there personally'.

'Will you be gone long?'

'A couple of days' Stephanie answered. 'I have a contact there who I think may be able to help me'.

Stephanie booked her flight to Singapore with a one night stay. It was the usual pattern of daylight flight northbound with an arrival late in the evening and then an overnight flight southbound the next night and home in time for breakfast. It was one of those trips, like to Bali or Fiji that most Australians take for granted and think nothing of. It was so different back home in Nottingham where some of the people who lived in the street she'd grown up in had never even been to France or Belgium or even Wales or Ireland. It was only after she'd left Britain that she understood just how insular some of her fellow Brits can be. They really didn't want to go anywhere if there was a danger of them not being able to get a 'proper' cup of tea or 'good old-fashioned English cooking'. Even one of her brothers who she would describe as a reasonably intelligent man wouldn't ever go anywhere on holiday if English wasn't the first language in the country concerned. It sometimes drove her sister-in-law mad.

She'd be gone barely thirty-six hours but she rushed over to Wayne's flat to meet him for sex. It had to be quick and Wayne delivered in his usual way but she walked away with a smile on her face and with some of him still dripping down the higher parts of her legs. He was getting better and improving all the time. She hadn't asked him what he'd done for sex when he was in prison. She didn't think she really wanted to know.

On her way to the airport she diverted to the suburb of Balmain for her last appointment before she left. It was at the Syrian consulate where she found the consulate secretary extremely helpful. He hinted that it wouldn't break his heart if the Assad regime at home fell and since he knew that Neil Jenkins' father, Yosef al-Ashwari had been an opponent of the regime, he was happy to do what he could.

Yosef al-Ashwari was a resident of Sydney from 1977 until 1982 under a working visa sponsored by St. Vincent's hospital at which he was opthalmics registrar. He returned to Damascus where he became involved in the underground opposition movement to the regime of the current President Assad's father and for his troubles he was imprisoned and brutally tortured during two periods in 1986 and 1988. Through a friendship he had with a member of the International Red Cross he managed to get himself and his family out of the country by crossing the border late at night into neighbouring Jordan and they finally settled in Switzerland where he went to work at a hospital in Zurich. It helped that he spoke good German as well as English and some French. Mariam al-Ashwari entered Australia three weeks before Neil Jenkins disappeared and there's no record of her having left again. To Stephanie it was further proof that the body found near Neil's car was that of his half-sister Mariam.

The consular secretary gave Stephanie the contact number's for Mariam al-Ashwari's brother and mother in Switzerland which was extraordinarily generous of him and he also confirmed to Stephanie that Yosef al-Ashwari had returned to Australia in the summer of 1991 but only stayed briefly for five days. This must've been when he visited Connie Weston to find out where Neil was and she refused to tell him. He also told her that the consulate had received no enquiries from the al-Ashwari family about Mariam al-Ashwari and why she hadn't returned home. Stephanie just couldn't get her head round that at all. After all, the consulate secretary pointed out that the entire family were all Swiss nationals now and had nothing to fear from contacting the Syrian authorities who their father had defected from.

After she'd left the consulate and was walking to her car she was approached by two police detectives holding up their badges. One was an early thirties woman who looked like a ball breaker with short blond hair and a black leather jacket over her t-shirt and jeans, and the other was just another white man in a suit.

'Miss Marshall? I'm detective Sonia Holness and this is my colleague detective Joe Buchan, both of the New South Wales police. Could we talk to you for a moment?'

'Well you'll need to be quick because I'm on my way to the airport'.

'Well this won't take long' said detective Holness. 'Are you investigating the disappearance of Neil Jenkins three years ago?'

'You know I am or else you wouldn't be here'.

'There's no need for hostility, Miss Marshall'.

'I wasn't being hostile' said Stephanie. 'But you were being over-sensitive'.

'I see' said Holness in measured tones. 'Well you should know that we've put out a warrant for the arrest of Neil Jenkins for the murder of Mariam al-Ashwari'.

'I thought you would. It would seem like the quickest way for you to say that you're on top of the case'.

'We're not on trial here, Miss Marshall'.

'Oh God, look I thought that new, brighter, younger officers like you in the police force would have a different attitude to private investigators like me. I thought you'd be more grown up and understand that we can help each other. But I see you're just as unreconstructed as any middle aged male officer with a beer gut who thinks women are only good for one thing. Now, if you'll excuse me'.

'Where are you flying to, Miss Marshall?' asked Buchan.

'None of your business but let me ask you something. Has it occurred to you that Neil Jenkins and his half-sister were the victims of an attack by robbers that night? Could it not have been that they shot Mariam but Neil managed to get away and just kept on running because he was in shock and then scared out of his wits? Or are you that desperate to paint Neil Jenkins as the killer of his sister who he'd only just come into contact with?'

'And for whom he must've held some deep resentments against' said Holness.

'That would lead him to murder? Don't you listen to his friends? People like Alan Ford or Patricia Palmer or Andy Green? They will all tell you that Neil Jenkins was no killer and yet here you are determined to make him one. Well I tell you this, I don't believe that Neil Jenkins is a murderer and certainly not a murderer of his own sister. My job is to find him on behalf of my client who wants to know what happened to her friend but beyond that I now want to prove his innocence'.

'Sounds like you're laying down a challenge to us, Miss Marshall'

'If you want to think that then be my guest but I bet I'll get to the truth before you do' Stephanie asserted. 'And whilst we're on the subject of the truth you might want to ask the original investigating officers on the case why they didn't check for footprints from the passenger side of Neil's car that night. Negligence or sheer bloody incompetence? You choose'.

The British Airways Boeing 777 aircraft pushed back from the stand at Sydney airport exactly on schedule at 3.40 pm. Stephanie had learned all the aviation industry speak when she'd dated an engineer who worked at the airport. She'd ended up going out with him for a couple of years in the end and they were happy mostly. Then she found out that he had horrendous gambling debts and he left the country one day, just like that, to avoid those of his

creditors who operated outside the law. There was also an ex-wife kicking around somewhere

taking him to court for non- payment of child maintenance. When she looked back Stephanie

could freely admit that sometimes she didn't half pick them. Now she was seeing an ex-con

who'd murdered his wife. She smiled to herself. Life never ceases to surprise.

When the bar trolley came round after take-off she took a gin and tonic and a little

flirtation with the steward meant that she was given two. She hadn't eaten since breakfast and

by the time the meal was presented to her she was feeling a little light headed. She still

managed a quarter bottle of red wine to accompany her lasagne and accepted a second bottle

from the steward who was now seriously flattering her. Stephanie liked a good flirt. She was

a Gemini and they were known for it. And this air steward who had a name badge on saying

'Patrick' was fit. He was about ten years younger than her and by the look of his shoulders

and upper arms it seemed like he must work out a lot at the gym. Still, she was only looking

and a girl can still window shop even if her credit card was up to its limit. But in any case,

Patrick was too pretty for her, too groomed, too prepared. It must go with the job she thought

but she liked her men to look a bit rougher than that. She liked stubble and the just got out of

bed look. Wayne did both of them really well.

She settled down to watch a film on her individual screen and from the large selection she

opted for some mindless Hollywood blockbuster caper starring Australia's own Hugh

Jackman. But she must've been tired because the next thing she knew they were coming

round with immigration landing cards for those leaving the flight in Singapore and not going

on to London and the Captain was making an announcement saying they'd be landing at

Singapore's Changi airport in thirty minutes. That was it. A seven and a half hour flight

almost gone. She went to the toilet and then picked up a black coffee from Patrick in the galley on the way back. He asked her what she'd be doing in Singapore and she told him she was going to be very busy whilst she was there and would hardly have a minute to herself. He got what she was trying to say and wished her a good stay.

In the taxi on the way to the hotel she was hungry again and decided that after she'd checked into the hotel she'd go down to Clarke Quay where there was one restaurant after another lined up next to the water and you could dine under the stars in the twenty-eight degree evening heat. The smells, the atmosphere, the location surrounded by skyscrapers, not to mention the heat, all added up to what Singapore meant to her. She'd been here a few times. She liked it. It was exotic but it was clean. And now she was going to enjoy it.

She deserved and needed a little time to herself. Work could wait until tomorrow.

FIONA THOMPSON EIGHT

Stephanie was always delighted to see her friend Ashraf at the Mallacca Bank in

Singapore. He was a proud Muslim, of Malaysian origin, a married man with five children

and he always treated Stephanie with the upmost courtesy and respect. She'd first met him

when he'd approached her on behalf of the bank because they needed some information on an

Australian citizen they suspected of fraud. They'd struck up a friendship that had lasted all

the years since and although she'd cashed in her favour chips many times it wasn't all one

way. She'd conducted several more investigations on Australian citizens for the Mallacca

bank. Some petty criminals think they're bigger than they are but the authorities somewhere

always catch up with them in the end. It's the big boys, the really serious criminals, who

always seem to end up getting away with it.

She was sitting in Ashraf's office on the ninth floor of the bank's headquarters and

drinking some much needed coffee. There wasn't much of a time change between Sydney

and Singapore but it was enough to have made her have to drag herself out of bed this

morning.

'So how are the family, Ashraf?'

'Oh they're growing up fast and costing me many, many sing dollars, Stephanie' Ashraf

replied, smiling. 'My eldest son is now in his second year at university in Edinburgh over in

Scotland. He's studying medicine as you know. He likes it over there'.

'Edinburgh is a beautiful city. I'm sure he's enjoying himself'.

'Yes, but my wife and I miss him very much. But that's life and the way it goes. Our

eldest daughter will be going off somewhere too next year. We seem to have intelligent

children'.

'Which is also a reflection on you and your wife, Ashraf'.

'Well I don't know about that but it's certainly a reflection on the Singapore education system' said Ashraf, modestly. He looked at the screen on his desktop computer. 'Now I received your email explaining what you needed and let's start with Patricia Palmer. She did take out three loans with us and she's been paying them back diligently, on time and there are no arrears on those accounts'.

'So where does it start to get interesting?'

'Well not with Patricia' said Ashraf. 'It certainly wasn't us who tipped off the Australian tax authorities about her. We responded to their enquiry but we didn't initiate it. And as for our dealings with her, like I say, everything is above board and there's nothing to tip off anybody about'.

'So what about Neil Jenkins?'

'Well, he opened an account with us shortly before the date on which you told me he disappeared and on the day he did disappear from Australia we received a total of six hundred thousand Australian dollars'.

'Yes that confirms what someone back home told me' said Stephanie. Her mind was racing with the possibilities of what she'd been told. 'But you talked just then about the day he disappeared from Australia. Why did you phrase it like that?'

Ashraf laughed. 'You don't miss a trick, Stephanie. You see, Neil Jenkins was here in Singapore two days after he disappeared from Australia'.

Stephanie sat up and took notice. 'To do what?'

'To transfer all the money in his account to another bank?'

'And is that other bank here in Singapore?'

'I'm afraid not' said Ashraf. 'He transferred the money to a bank in Thailand'.

'Thailand? Why there?'

'That's something I can't tell you, Stephanie. But I think it does prove that he was still alive then and he had some intent to go somewhere and do something. As to where and what that could be, who can say?'

Stephanie returned to her hotel to take stock. It was on days like these when she envied all the sensible people with sensible jobs who were lying by the pool with a beer and a plate of Indonesian Nasi Goreng. But she didn't have a sensible job. She had one where the job description seemed to shift quicker than grains of drifting sand. First Patricia Palmer seemed like a genuine woman concerned for her friend who'd disappeared in highly dramatic and unusual circumstances whereas she was actually about as sincere as the Queen was after the death of Princess Diana. Then Neil Jenkins who'd been described as a bloody good bloke by everyone who knew him except for his own mother, turns out to be someone who was hiding a half-sister from some of his best friends and half a million dollars that he transferred overseas on the day he disappeared. How could he have not known about the money that was clearly being laundered through his account? How could Patricia have hidden that from him?

Before she did anything else she decided to call Mariam al-Ashwari's family in Zurich. She sat on the end of her bed and dialed the number that had been given her by the Syrian consulate secretary in Sydney and it was answered after only a couple of rings. It was a young sounding voice and she took it to be Mariam's brother.

'Hello?'

'Oh yes, hello, my name is Stephanie Marshall and I'd like to speak to a member of the al-Ashwari family, please?'

The voice on the other end was sharp. 'What is your business with them?'

'I'm a private investigator based in Sydney, Australia, and it's with regard to ... '

Whoever was on the other end hung up before Stephanie had the chance to finish. Not wishing to be deterred Stephanie rang the number again.

'What do you want with us?' the voice demanded.

'I'm really not your enemy'.

'I'll be the judge of that'.

'Look, I was employed by my client to look into the disappearance of Neil Jenkins and it's through that investigation that I learned of Mariam al-Ashwari. Are you Touma al-Ashwari? Mariam's brother?'

'So what if I am'.

'Well I'm sure you know that Neil Jenkins was your half-brother and ... '

Touma laughed sardonically down the line. 'Don't you even think of associating that pervert with my family. Do you hear me? Don't you even think it'

'So you are Touma?'

'I am the brother of Mariam, yes. That much I will admit to. But as for that half breed so-called brother I have nothing but contempt'.

'Isn't that a little harsh?'

'Harsh? He perverted the laws of God by sleeping with other men. It's disgusting. No good Muslim should have anything to do with that kind. He will burn in Hell for the rest of eternity'.

That's funny, thought Stephanie. All the fundamentalist Christians say the same thing about gay people. Nothing to seperate religious extremists of any kind as far as Stephanie was concerned. They were all mad whichever 'side' they claimed to represent.

'And what about your sister Mariam?'

'What about her?'

'Well haven't you wondered why she never came home?'

'She made her bed'.

'Excuse me?'

'Isn't that what you say in your country?'

'Mr. al-Ashwari, I ... '

' ... look, Miss private investigator. Both Mariam and my father were secular Muslims who betrayed the very foundation of Islam by reaching out and tolerating other faiths. That is not my way. My way is to apply the Koran and the teachings of the blessed prophet without compromise and in fear of God. Mariam was always a Daddy's girl. She could always accept the secular way of living. She walked around in western clothes like some slut and she disgraced the blessed prophet over and over again'.

'In what way?'

'By conforming to Western values. She would sit round a table and have dinner with men. If we'd have been brought up as proper Muslims she would've had to have asked our father before she did that and if he'd have acted like a proper Muslim father then he'd have refused her permission. She went down to Australia to trace that half-breed because she thought it was the fair thing to do and because my father had asked her to. He knew what my reaction would've been if he'd asked me which is why he didn't. But he and Mariam had been corrupted by the west. They had abandoned the Muslim cause'.

'So you had no time for bringing your brother in from the cold?'

'He's not my brother!'

'Oh so is he still alive?'

'His very existence sent a dagger through my mother's heart and yet even she thought that the half breed deserved something from my father's estate'.

'Your father was obviously a wealthy man. Half a million dollars is a generous settlement. But tell me, why didn't you try and find your sister when she didn't return to Switzerland?'

'Because … because it's none of your business'.

'Was it because you resented her for trying to find Neil and give him what he deserved? Does all this morality I hear from you really mask a pretty selfish and cunning individual inside?'

'Allah will be my judge'.

'You didn't want to share the money'.

'It has nothing to do with money!'

'Then you tell me what it is about, Mr. al-Ashwari'.

'I don't have to tell you anything'.

'Well what about your mother?'

'Leave her out of it'.

'Didn't she want to know what had happened to her daughter?'

'How dare you pry into our family business like this'.

'Unless she knew all along what had happened to her?'

'Just be careful before you go way too far'.

'You see it's been puzzling me why the hospital where your sister Mariam worked didn't even make even the most basic of enquiries to find out what might have happened to her. But it's just struck me that perhaps it was because they knew'.

'You're being ridiculous. How would they know?'

'Because either you or your mother had told them'.

'You're a fantasist'.

'Do you know what happened to Mariam, Mr. al-Ashwari?'

'Watch your stupid mouth'.

'Well shall I put it another way?'

'You can put it however many ways you like'.

'Did you set things up to make it look like Neil Jenkins had murdered his own sister?'

The line went dead.

When you're an investigator an open thread is something you can't resist pulling at until
the thread unwinds and pulls everything apart. The more she thought about it the more it
made perfect sense. The al-Ashwari family were behind Neil Jenkins disappearance and
somehow either Mariam was part of it too or, and this was more likely in Stephanie's mind,
she got caught in the middle of whatever her brother had planned. She called the Syrian
consulate in Sydney and asked the question as to whether Touma al-Ashwari had been in
Australia three years ago in the weeks before Neil Jenkins had disappeared. The answer was
that he hadn't been but that didn't mean anything. He could've come in under a false passport
and if he was planning on committing some kind of criminal act then that's probably what he
had done. Now it was a question of trying to convince the police that Touma al-Ashwari had
been involved but that wasn't going to be easy considering that Ashraf at the bank had
revealed that Neil Jenkins had been in Singapore two days after he disappeared from
Australia and transferred his money to another bank in Thailand. It made it look like he was

on the run. Stephanie was convinced he wasn't. But if he wasn't then what was he doing and where was he now?

There was one more person Stephanie had to see before she left Singapore. Kevin Lee should've been someone with whom she had some regard. But she couldn't stand the little creep. He was a private investigator like herself but that's where the similarities ended as far as Stephanie was concerned.

She'd arranged to meet him in a sandwich bar which was on street level of the Raffles shopping center. It was easy to get there from her hotel because the metro station formed an interchange between various lines and it all added to the air of effortless efficiency Stephanie always found in Singapore. On top of the shopping center was the highest hotel in Asia with his 70-storey circular block forming part of the city skyline. Stephanie had never stayed there because it was way too expensive for her personal or professional pocket but she had been to the top storey bar for drinks and the view from up there was breathtaking.

She'd just bitten into a chicken and avocado sandwich in ciabatta bread when Kevin turned up. He had an affected swagger that almost made her laugh out loud. He seemed to see himself as a Chinese Jack Reacher from the Lee Child books. He was all ray-ban aviator sunglasses, gelled hair, and a leather jacket even in thirty-two degrees of heat. What a fucking twat. But useful.

'So, Steph, what brings you to town?'

'You really should stop watching all those old American movies, Kevin. Your script is really suffering because of it'.

'What can I tell you?' he asked with his hands and arms expanded. 'I suit the dialogue'.

'Whatever' said Stephanie who was still trying not to laugh. 'I need you to trace the movements of someone for me'.

'Who?'

'His name is Neil Jenkins' said Stephanie who handed Kevin a photograph of Neil from her handbag. 'He's an Australian citizen and he was here three years ago after which I've reason to believe he moved on to Thailand' She went on to explain everything else about Neil's disappearance. 'I need a conclusion to this as quickly as you can, Kevin. I'll pay you out of what my client pays me'.

'Yes, yes, usual arrangement, no problem, Stephanie' said Kevin as he stared thoughtfully at the photograph. 'Is money shifting something to do with it?'

'Yes' said Stephanie. 'From Australia to here to Thailand. Can you use your contacts in Bangkok to see where he went once he got there?'

'Sure thing' said Kevin.

Stephanie handed him a file with all the details about Neil that she'd just been explaining.

'This looks straight forward but you never know until you dive in' said Kevin. 'What do you think he spent the money on?'

'Gaining a new identity' said Stephanie. 'And that's where you'll really have your work cut out because he had more than enough money to bury his original self very deep'.

That night Stephanie caught the British Airways flight home as it came through Singapore on the way from London to Sydney. It was quite a novelty to hear so many British accents and she quite liked it. The crew were all girls so there was no 'Patrick' to flirt with but her tried and tested formula of gin and tonic followed by red wine did the trick again and she was asleep not long after they'd taken her dinner tray away. Bollocks to all the trendy greenie control freak health crap about drinking lots of water on planes and avoiding alcohol. All that meant was that you stayed awake all night. Well she'd rather sleep than sit there sipping frequently from a bottle of water and pretending to be oh so fucking virtuous.

A couple of cups of black coffee before the plane landed and by the time she got into her car to drive home she felt reasonably okay. So she decided to surprise Wayne and call on him on her way. She checked her watch and by the time she got to Fiona Thompson House in Manly it would be about half six. He normally had a dawn horn in the morning. It must have something to do with the sun coming up.

She stopped off at a café to pick up a couple of pastries and then headed round to Fiona Thompson House. She parked outside and couldn't resist a smile as she walked up to Wayne's door at the back of the house. She hadn't phoned because she wanted to retain the element of surprise. She knocked and was full of anticipation. She knocked again and she could hear movement inside. Then the door opened and Wayne stood there in his bathrobe, his hairy chest prominent in the gap and very alluring. But what was the look on his face all about?

'Hi' said Stephanie.

'You didn't call' said Wayne.

'I thought I'd surprise you?' said Stephanie. 'Sorry, have I done the wrong thing?'

'No … that's good'.

Stephanie stepped into the tiny flat as her spirits started to sink. 'Wayne, what's wrong? Aren't you pleased to see me?'

'Of course I'm pleased to see you'.

'But?'

At that moment the door to Wayne's bedroom opened and a woman of about Stephanie's age came out in a short black lace nightdress. She looked sleepy. She drifted past Stephanie on the way to the toilet.

'I'm Jill' she said. 'Jill O'Donnell. I'm an old friend of Wayne's and this really is not what you might be thinking. Don't look so shocked. You're an understanding woman of the world according to big boy here and I'll leave him to explain'.

Stephanie watched Jill disappear into the toilet and then turned to Wayne. 'Well, big boy? Do you want to test how understanding I am?'

'Come through and we'll talk' said Wayne as he led Stephanie through to the living room where they both sat down. 'I wish you'd take that look off your face, Stephanie'.

'Oh I'm sorry if it makes you feel uncomfortable but tough! I was so excited when I hatched the idea to drive over here from the airport and surprise you. I thought that all I had to do was slide into bed beside you and you'd welcome me home. I never thought you'd take up with someone else as soon as my back was turned'.

'I haven't taken up with someone else, Stephanie'.

'Oh so Jill is just a mirage is she?'

'No, I'm a prostitute' said Jill as she stepped into the small hallway. 'I've been a prostitute off and on for thirty odd years. I met Wayne during one of my off periods a very long time ago but it didn't work out. But I'm the only one who ever visited him in prison and I'm a busy woman. I run an escort agency down in Melbourne, all legal and above board. I've got seven girls working for me plus four guys who look after women and three guys who look after the gays. Some of my girls are not averse to some lesbian action too so I've got all angles covered. Wayne asked me to come here for a reason but I'm going to let him explain all that. My flight back to Melbourne isn't until two this afternoon so I'm going back to bed for some more shut eye. I'll see you later'.

Jill disappeared back into the bedroom and Stephanie looked at Wayne not knowing what the hell was going to come out next. But despite the circumstances and the situation she kind of liked Jill. She was honest and upfront. She didn't appear to be hiding behind anything.

'I thought Jill was the one years ago' said Wayne. 'Then along came Patricia's son John who captured Jill's heart. It kind of killed things off between us'.

'So what provoked the reconciliation?'

'Stephanie, I asked Jill here because of you'.

'Because of me?'

'You're the best thing that's happened to me in a very long time. I want everything between us to be absolutely perfect and that includes sex. I asked Jill here so she could remind me of a few ways to satisfy a woman that I might've forgotten about during all those years in prison. I just want to please you. That really is what it was all about, Stephanie'.

'You asked a prostitute to help you with our sex life? I suppose I should be flattered'.

'You believe me then?'

'Well of course I believe you'.

Wayne knelt down at Stephanie's feet and took hold of her hands. 'I just didn't think I deserved you and I wanted to show you how much I've come to care about you over this short time. Sex is one thing, Stephanie. But sex within a relationship is something different altogether. I want you to feel everything a woman should feel from a man, Stephanie. I don't want you to miss out on anything because you're with me and not some other bloke who hasn't been inside like I have'.

Stephanie reached out and Wayne laid himself down on the sofa and rested his head in Stephanie's lap. She gently stroked the side of his face and let him talk.

'When I first went inside I couldn't get over the enormity of what I'd done. I'd killed someone. I'd committed the greatest taboo and yet the world hadn't stopped spinning. It was all contained within my own little world and somehow I had to survive. I had to survive prison which was darker than anything I'd ever know. I became convinced that the authorities monitored all those of us on life sentences so they could needle us when we were at our most vulnerable because you have no control in prison. You're completely under the control of the authorities and I know that's what prison is about but it does tend to fuck with your head. I invented all kinds of conspiracies that were pointless and ridiculous but that's what it does to you. But I made it worse by refusing the chance of parole. I'd killed Susan and doing the right thing was more important to me than even my own freedom. I know Beryl and David wouldn't believe that, even after all these years, but it's true. I couldn't see an identity for myself beyond those walls. I was too full of guilt and yet I raged at the other prisoner's hypocrisy. They attack sex offenders and yet rapists are never touched. Don't get me wrong, I'm not saying that we should be soft on sex offenders but the prisoners own code when it came to that sort of thing just sucked. But then when I was released I just didn't know who I was. Andy took me to the movies and I couldn't stand the darkness because in prison that's when all the scores were settled and you never really knew if they were going to be knocking on your door. I had almost every bone in my body broken at one time or another. Not so much towards the end because I became this kind of senior figure who all the other prisoners came to when they needed support of one kind or another. But past experiences stayed with me'.

'Wayne, you've got to make the decision to move on from that dark place'.

'I know but don't you see?' Wayne pleaded as the tears rolled down his face. 'You're part of that. That's why I had to make everything as right as I could'.

'And that's where Jill came in'.

'She's not a bad person, Stephanie'.

'I can see that'.

'And she was the only one who came to visit me in prison. Our romantic connection ended years ago but we are firm friends. I should've turned to her when I was having all the problems with Susan and she might've helped me and stopped it all happening, who knows. Please don't hate me for having her come round, Stephanie. I couldn't stand it if you hated me'.

'I don't hate you for it, Wayne'.

'I just want to be the man, you know. I want so much to please you'.

'Then don't try so hard'.

'I couldn't help myself'.

'But Wayne, sex is something we work out together, just the two of us as part of who we are as a couple. I know it's been difficult for you but I'm here and I'm not planning on going anywhere else. And the earth doesn't have to move every night'.

Jill woke up a while later and had a shower. She then got dressed and went into the living room where Stephanie was reading the morning paper and drinking some coffee.

'Where's Wayne?'

'He's had to go and do a job at one of the other properties. He's coming straight back'

'Stephanie, I'm really sorry you had to walk in on that'.

'Well it wasn't the homecoming I'd hoped for but never mind'.

'You understood in the end then?'

'Yes' said Stephanie. 'I did'.

'Well Wayne's lucky because some women would've totally freaked out'.

'It was a shock more than anything' said Stephanie. 'And as for anything else I'm not in a position to throw stones. My sons grew up on the other side of the world without me and it was entirely my doing'.

'That's remarkably candid'.

'I detest hypocrisy'.

'Boy, Wayne really has struck gold'.

'Jill, you and Wayne are old friends. Why don't you sit down and tell me about yourself?'

Jill sat down in the armchair and crossed her legs casually. 'I nearly married Wayne once' she admitted. 'But his scheming ways back then caught up with him and we didn't. I was engaged to his step-brother John too but I had to call that off when one of his friends turned out to be an ex client. You see, I've been on the game more or less all my adult life but I was trying to keep on the straight and narrow back then. Anyway then I did get married to a wonderful Irishman called Brian who turned out to be involved with the IRA back in Belfast. We're talking the eighties at the height of the troubles over there. He was killed trying to avenge the death of his brother. It's funny but I still think about him every day'.

'The one that could've been but never was'.

'Yeah, something like that. I think we could've been happy but … oh well, that's life and that's death and you can't cheat either of them. Perhaps I was just never meant to be in a normal relationship with someone. Whether it was John, Wayne, Brian, or Robin or Alan who came afterwards, something always happened to pull us apart. I never got a shot at lasting happiness. So I gave up in the end. I've been single now for years'.

'Wayne says you have a daughter?'

Jill's face lit up. 'Oh yeah, Fee, short for Fiona. She's an English teacher would you believe? I mean, how did I manage that? She lives with her boyfriend not far from where I am'.

'And her father?'

'His name was Terry. He raped me. That's how I got pregnant. The problem was he was the son of my best friend, Fiona Thompson who used to own this place. She'd been a reformed high class call girl from back in the fifties and she took me in one day like she took in so many waifs and strays and helped them. Talk about the tart with the heart. Anyway, she persuaded me not to get rid of her grandchild so I had her and after the disasters with Robin and Alan which I won't bore you with now, Fiona talked me into making a go of it with Terry and we did try for a while but I didn't love him and I couldn't get past what he'd done. I mean, there's a big difference between paying a girl for sex and raping her. My girls, and boys, are in total control of what they do and I back them one hundred percent'.

'What happened to Terry?'

'He drifted off somewhere. I don't know where he went but I haven't seen him for years. That's when I went back into the business. It was all I could do. I couldn't turn to anybody because there was nobody there. Wayne was in prison and John had moved up to Queensland

and anyway we'd finished way before that. I was alone with a kid and I had no money. Fiona had died. It's a classic really'.

'Sounds like you've done a bloody good job considering she's an English teacher'.

'Yeah, I'm pretty proud' said Jill, smiling. 'I sometimes don't know if I'd have made it through life if I hadn't had her to take care of though. Does that make sense?'

'Perfectly. Just the promise of seeing my boys has sometimes got me through some pretty dark times. So I take it you're successful at the escort business?'

'Yeah, we do okay actually. We have slack times when it seems like everyone stays at home and pleasures themselves rather than going out and paying for somebody else to do it. But we have some top end clients as well as ordinary men and women and then we have companies who pay us to entertain potential clients for them. Some of that goes right up to government department level'.

'You don't surprise me'.

'It would make you hair curl if you knew what went on to secure contracts in this great country of ours. Actually, I don't think it would because I don't think anything would really surprise you'.

Stephanie laughed. 'I'll take that as a compliment'.

'Then of course I've got my sideline company and that consistently makes money for me'.

'What's the sideline?'

'Sexy lingerie' Jill revealed. 'The company is called Silky Secrets. We're online and everything'.

Stephanie's jaw dropped. 'Jill, there's something I must ask you'.

'What? You're looking all serious all of a sudden'.

'Have you had any business dealings with Patricia Palmer in recent years?'

Jill felt rather uncomfortable. She didn't want to talk about Patricia but now she'd mentioned the name of her lingerie business she had no choice.

'I've let something slip there' said Jill. 'No pun intended'.

'Money was being passed by Patricia Palmer through the bank account of Neil Jenkins shortly before he disappeared that went to the account of your company, Silky Secrets. Now what was all that about Jill? I'm sorry but you're going to have to tell me the truth'

Stephanie drove round to Patricia and David's Darling harbor apartment and she was determined to have it out with the woman who seemed to throw her shadow over almost everything to do with this case.

Patricia stubbed out her seventh cigarette of the morning in the ashtray on the low table between the two long white leather sofas.

'Is David here?' asked Stephanie.

'No, he had to go back to the farm to attend to things there'.

'Patricia, you haven't been entirely straight with me, have you?'

Patricia squared up to her. 'Who's been telling tales?'

'I didn't need anyone to tell any tales' said Stephanie. 'The facts just seemed to slip out of everywhere and they all have your name on them'.

Patricia sat down on the sofa. 'Well, you'd better tell me how these so-called facts have misinformed you about me. Now please, sit down'.

Stephanie sat down beside Patricia. 'Is the real reason you want to find Neil because you want to recover the hundred thousand dollars he whipped from you before he disappeared?'

'I am facing financial ruin if the tax authorities have their way, Stephanie'.

'I'll take that as a yes'.

'But Stephanie I swear I want to know what happened too' Patricia pleaded. 'Especially as the police seem determined to say that he's a murderer'.

'Yes, well he isn't'.

'You know that for sure?'

'No, not for sure but let's say I'm ninety-nine percent certain he didn't murder Mariam al-Ashwari'.

'Then if he didn't who did?'

'I have my thoughts but I'm going to keep them to myself until I can check them out further. But I have other priorities to ask you about like why you were passing money through Neil's account and into the account of a company called Silky Secrets?'

'How did you know about that?'

'Never mind how I know, Patricia. I want to know what was going on? I want to know why you were challenning money from the Ramberg corporation through Neil and on to Silky Secrets?'

'I'd been a director of the Ramberg corporation for years. Three years ago the company was in deep financial strife. We'd overstretched ourselves and the cash flow was approaching a cliff edge. We were bidding for a contract from Donaldson Holdings that would guarantee our financial future. They were offering us the chance to support them in the maintenance of all federal civil aviation sites right across the country. I knew Jill O'Donnell. We'd been associated in the past and I knew her line of business. So I contacted her and we came up with a plan to help Ramberg get the Donaldson account'.

'Using sex as a bribe?'

'Oh don't look down your nose, Stephanie. I know you're not naïve and you can well imagine that it happens all the time in business'.

'I'm not looking down my nose, Patricia. I was just clarifying things'.

'Sorry. It just looked like you were. Anyway look, some of Jill's girls, and boys in a couple of cases, were used to seduce those members of the Donaldson board we needed to secure the vote going our way and we threatened them with exposure if they didn't. It worked. We got the Donaldson account and the Ramberg corporation has lived happily ever after. But I hid the money trail because, for obvious reasons, I didn't want anyone to find proof that we'd fixed things that way. Hiding the money by routing it through Neil's account was easy. I managed to get his access codes and account numbers'.

'How on earth did you do that?'

'I had a key to his apartment of course because I'm the owner. I went in one day when he was at work and got the information from his personal files'.

'No bloody wonder he was pissed off with you'

'Yes, I know. He found out the day he disappeared and he was absolutely furious. He said he felt betrayed and that I'd let him down, which of course I had. But I couldn't have asked him if I could do it because I couldn't risk him saying no. That's how serious it all was'.

Stephanie was relieved that Patricia's version of events regarding Ramberg and the Donaldson account chimed exactly with what Jill had told her. But that didn't mean she didn't think there were other hidden mine shafts waiting to for the truth to fall down.

'I need that hundred thousand back, Stephanie. If the tax authorities close me down I need to know I've still got money that David and I can start again with. Yes, I used Neil, someone I thought the world of, but I was desperate. If Ramberg had gone down it would've taken thousands of my money with it. Neil would've probably understood but like I said, I couldn't take that risk. I've always had a strong sense of my own survival'.

Stephanie stood up and paced round the room. 'I just wish you'd told me this at the start'.

'Stephanie, I'm sorry, but you've got to understand my position. I was fighting then and I'm fighting now and if I've been less than honest with you then that's why. But I'm not as black and white as people paint me'.

'You just want your money back'.

'And my friend' Patricia emphasized. 'I want Neil back too'.

'He was in Singapore three days after he disappeared from Palm Beach' Stephanie revealed.

'Oh my God, really? But how did he get there? And why did he run?'

'Well, all the money that he transferred there on the day he disappeared, including your hundred thousand, was transferred again only this time to a bank in Thailand. That's where I'm focusing now along with who killed Mariam al-Ashwari because I feel they will hold a major key to this whole investigation'.

'You said before you think you have some idea about who did kill Mariam al-Ashwari?'

'I do' said Stephanie. 'But you'll also remember that I said I wanted to investigate further before I let all that out. Now I'm asking you, Patricia? Is there anything else that you haven't told me about that I should know?'

Patricia shook her head. 'No, there isn't'.

'Are you sure? Because I could be getting into dangerous stuff here and I need to be armed with as much information as I can get'.

'No, there's nothing else' said Patricia, lying through her teeth. 'I promise you that'.

English wasn't as widely or as fluently spoken in Bangkok as it was in Singapore. But Stephanie found the Thai people charming. They were all so eager to please and seemed to really want a visitor to feel welcome in their country. It had been an almost nine hour flight up from Sydney because of a head wind and she negotiated her way onto a coach heading for the city. It was getting late. It was not far off midnight but Bangkok was one of those cities that never seemed to rest and the lights were on in buildings all the way into town. Stephanie wanted to rest though. It was a three hour time change with Sydney and not only was she physically tired but the flight had been a bit of a trial. She'd had a great meal. A lovely Thai green curry with chicken that actually tasted like what it claimed to be, but the flight had been full and she'd been stuck next to two very tall young Danish guys who were making a connecting flight in Bangkok for Copenhagen. They were nice enough and quite amusing in their way, polite, friendly guys who any mother would be proud of, their English was excellent and Stephanie was able to talk to them about her fondness for Scandinavian crime novels and TV series. But they didn't seem to recognize the signals she gave out when she just wanted a bit of peace. They had to give her chapter and bloody verse all about their 'most wonderful' time in Australia where they'd seen the giant saltwater crocodiles in the Northern Territories and climbed up Ayers rock to name but two of their many adventures over the three weeks they'd been there. They liked their beer too and the serene like stewardesses on Thai Airways were very attentive to these two blond Scandinavian hunks.

The next morning she went and had a breakfast of chilled slices of papaya with toast and coffee in the hotel restaurant which was on the second floor. It offered a panoramic view of the city but Stephanie had no idea which part of Bangkok she was in. It was such a vast city and getting her bearings was beyond her brain. She hoped that she'd be able to do a little light shopping whilst she was there. Bangkok is a shoppers' paradise and she was thinking of maybe a couple of shirts for Wayne and some for her sons James and Matthew. The best time to 'do' the markets was at night and she'd got an open return ticket. The Sydney flights left in the evening so she'd have to think carefully about her schedule to be able write in some retail time before she heads home.

She took a taxi round to the Royal Thai bank and like with most public buildings in very hot and humid countries, she was hit by a wall of air-conditioning as soon as she went through the automatic doors. To cool down was a welcome relief from the outside heat but it was pretty cold. No wonder all the staff seemed to be wearing jackets or cardigans.

Patricia had given her a generous sum with which to get around any secrecy policies the bank may have or any reluctance on the part of the banking staff to get around any obstacles with some imagination. But as it turned out no such incentives were needed. Thanks to the advance work of Kevin Lee back in Singapore the Royal Thai bank had got it into their head that Stephanie was representing the Australian government on official business. Well who was she to contradict them? They didn't even ask her for ID. Well, she wasn't really committing any major crime. Many members of the Australian civil service had failed miserably at impersonating a human being and they always got away with it.

But any risk of potential law breaking, however flimsy and insignificant it was, shot right out of Stephanie's mind when she learned what had happened to Neil Jenkins' money after it had been transferred here from Singapore. A small amount of it, barely twenty thousand dollars, had been transferred to the Chonburi clinic. Not entirely significant on the face of it. The clinic was located in the city of Chonburi, about eighty kilometers east of Bangkok and the name meant 'City of Water'. But it was what the clinic specialized in that fired up

Stephanie's interest. It was a gender reaffirmation clinic. It was where men went for surgery to change them into being a woman.

Stephanie thought it would be best to take a taxi out to Chonburi. The driver had been recommended by her hotel and she took it as given that he wouldn't drive her down some jungle track and force himself on her. Then she chastised herself. She was being a stupid neurotic bitch. She was also being racist. If a hotel in Sydney had made the same kind of recommendation she wouldn't bat an eyelid. So why was she looking at it any differently just because she was in Thailand? She would really begin to hate herself if she turned into one of those women who believe every man to be a potential rapist, especially if he had a skin that wasn't white.

She looked out at the paddy fields as she went by. The trees, the dirt tracks, the squared off fields where rice was growing and providing an income for the local people. That was unless it all went to multi nationals based in Australia or America or somewhere in Europe. She saw a lot of children in the fields. It was only eleven o'clock in the morning. They should all be at school.

When she arrived at the Chonburi clinic it was the pristine appearance of it that struck her most. The façade was covered in two tones of marble, a light purple mixed with a yellowish cream. It looked more like a hotel than somewhere men went to have their tackle inverted. It was at the top of a hill and then back down it a little and it was surrounded by immaculately kept gardens. Maybe the serenity was needed by men in the position of wanting to truly change their lives. The more she thought about it the more she wouldn't be at all surprised if Neil Jenkins had been a patient here. A man who was attracted to other men but who didn't feel gay? A man who was as uncomfortable about being part of the gay world as he was about being part of the straight one? Stephanie hadn't come across many transsexuals in her time but as far as Neil Jenkins was concerned the pieces were all starting to fall into place.

She strode confidently into reception on a high that came from believing she was beginning to work some of it all out. The manager at the bank in Bangkok had called the clinic to make her appointment and the medical director was waiting for her in his office. This was further down the hill from reception and she was escorted down there by a young woman who was way too thin and gorgeous but Stephanie forgave her.

The medical director was a man called Professor Preecha Attakonpan and was a middle-aged man of average height with a rather jolly round face and black hair with streaks of grey. He was wearing what looked like a well made light grey shirt that was finished off with a silk tie that didn't look like it had come off one of the market stalls. His suit was dark grey and his jacket was hanging over the back of his leather desk chair.

'Please sit down, Miss Marshall and tell me how I can help you'.

'Well' said Stephanie. 'It's about someone who I believe may have been a patient of yours around three years ago. His name is Neil Jenkins, age thirty-one and an Australian citizen'.

'Well of course we do get a lot of people through our doors from all parts of the world to take advantage of our surgery techniques and our location far away from home'.

'He was of mixed race' Stephanie explained as she handed him one of the several photographs she had of Neil. 'His mother was a white Australian and his father was Syrian. Here's a picture of him'.

'A fine looking young man' said the doctor.

'Yes he is'.

'And why are you wanting to track him down?'

'He disappeared from a small coastal town just north of Sydney three years ago in rather dramatic circumstances. His friends are worried about him and one of them in particular asked me to investigate'.

'I see'.

'So do you remember him?'

'Miss Marshall, you must appreciate I'm sure that at this clinic we have to be especially discreet'.

'Of course I do'.

'And that any breach of that discretion would potentially damage our reputation and therefore our business'.

'I understand entirely, doctor'.

'But I feel that I can indeed trust you'

Stephanie breathed an inward sigh of relief. This doctor may be charming but it was starting to feel a bit like pulling teeth. But then he qualified his appraisal.

The doctor leaned back in his chair and brought his hands together with his two index fingers pointing upwards. 'I think you'll find that the fortune you seek will follow a donation to our children's school which is in the building next door'.

'Oh?'

'Yes' said the doctor. 'We take young girls and boys, some as young as seven or eight years old, who've been sold into the sex trade in Bangkok by their parents who are extremely poor and desperate for money. We buy them back and nurture them into being little girls and boys again who can trust the adults around them'.

'That seems very laudable'.

'Yes it is. And there are so many. My country doesn't like to advertise the obvious social problems we face'.

'A thousand Australian dollars?'

'That would be very generous' said the doctor. 'Make all the necessary arrangements with my secretary and she will then take you to meet the principal of the school'.

'And Neil Jenkins?'

'Be patient, Miss Marshall' said the doctor. 'The information you seek will come to you. I said the very same thing to the other Australian lady who was here looking for Neil Jenkins just a few weeks ago'.

'Which other Australian lady?'

'Her name was Beryl Hamilton' the doctor revealed. 'She is from Melbourne I believe. I'm surprised the bank in Bangkok didn't tell you about her since it was they who sent her here just like they sent you'.

Well, well, well thought Stephanie. What a cat to set amongst the pigeons. Patricia's old sworn enemy on the chase of Patricia's lost old friend. But what the hell would Beryl

Hamilton have to gain from any of this? Could it have been her who dobbed Patricia in to the tax authorities? What had Patricia done to rattle this Beryl Hamilton? She knew that they were old foes but she thought that was all over years ago. Stone the bloody crows, thought Stephanie. Getting involved with this group of people was like stepping into a pit of snakes. You never knew where the next bite was going to come from.

She organized the bank transfer with the doctor's secretary who then walked her through the gardens that separated the clinic from the school. The closer she got the louder the kids voices became. It must be break time. The sprinklers that were spraying the garden with a soft stream of water was catching her a little as she walked by. It was very refreshing.

The secretary left Stephanie at the door to what looked like an extremely tidy office. The woman sitting at the computer with her back to Stephanie had long black hair that just covered her shoulders and Stephanie could see that her nails were painted the deepest red. She was dressed in a plain white t-shirt and a pair of faded blue jeans. She turned and Stephanie had to take a sharp intake of breath even though she wasn't really surprised.

'I'm Elaine Johnson, school principal. What can I do for you?'

'I'm looking for Neil Jenkins'.

'Neil Jenkins doesn't exist anymore' said Elaine. 'But I can tell you anything you need to know about him'.

'Why did he run away? Who killed his half-sister? What was Beryl Hamilton doing here?'

Elaine paused and then said 'This is not the place to talk about these things. I'm due a break. There's a café just down the road. Let's go there'.

FIONA THOMPSON ELEVEN

They sat down in the small brightly lit café which was in a busy street with people walking and going up and down on motorcycles all the time. Stephanie was thankful when Elaine ordered a cheeseburger and fries. It was just what she fancied too and she ordered the same. She liked Thai food but she got bored with it very quickly and if truth be told she preferred Indian.

'Do you like living here?' asked Stephanie.

'Yes, I do' Elaine answered. 'I've found peace here. I've found a purpose to my life that I never knew before'.

'Are you talking in terms of all your life? I mean, when you were Neil Jenkins as well as who you are now?'

'You show great sensitivity, Stephanie. I'm grateful. And the answer to your question is all my life, before and after'.

'And that's because of working here at the school?'

'Yes' said Elaine. 'You wouldn't believe the lives these kids have had. Thailand is a beautiful country full of beautiful people but like with everywhere else there are contradictions. The country has got one of the fastest growing economies in the world just now but it still means that those at the top are getting richer and there's a growing middle class that's creaming most of everything else up leaving a whole mass of people at the bottom who are being left out of all the economic progress'.

'Capitalism at its best'.

'Yeah, that's a way of putting it'.

'How does this place survive financially?'

'We're a charity. I've invested a lot of money into it but we're dependent on donations. We've got ninety-two kids here at the moment. We're twinned with schools in the UK, Germany, and America. They fundraise for us and although it gets a bit close at times we manage to survive. We also get a grant from the Thai government who like to help us on the quiet because the reason why these kids come to us is embarrassing to them and we use that grant to pay for the teachers. We also have English teachers too from Britain, Ireland, Canada, the US, Australia, and New Zealand. We have to survive for the sake of the kids we save. Their parents never had anything and never will because the whole system has always been stacked against them. But we've got to break that cycle. We've got to give these kids hope in a better future'.

'How do you rescue them?'

'We go into Bangkok at night and we literally take them off the streets'.

'Isn't that a little dangerous?'

'It can be' said Elaine. 'Some of the gangs who control them can get a little physical but we've got our own muscle too'.

'You seem very committed to your work here'.

'It's the injustice of it all, Stephanie. It's the unfairness. If the country is growing then the whole country should benefit from it and not have to give themselves to all the disgusting paedophiles who don't come here for the beaches and the shopping. The kids are raped and sexually assaulted time and time again in what becomes a living hell for them. Lives destroyed before they're even teenagers. Its' part of the way of life here and everybody turns a blind eye but nobody would if it was happening in Australia so why is it okay for it to happen here? Why do people shrug their shoulders and say its' all part of what goes on in a country like this? A country like this? How fucking arrogant is that? Children in countries like Australia are no more entitled to a safe, happy childhood with people who love them than children are here. All children deserve the best that the world can give them, no matter where they've been born'.

'I agree' said Stephanie. 'But I'm not sure everyone back home would agree with you'.

'Oh I watched the election coverage and I cringed at some of the ranting against immigration. But let's face it, unless you're an aborigine in Australia then everyone is part of the immigrant community. We're all descended from people who went there from other parts of the world, some of them fleeing from war and persecution and some, like the new Prime Minister himself, an economic migrant from somewhere like the UK'.

'That's what I was when I first arrived'.

'So you'll know what I'm talking about' said Elaine. 'And no offence, Stephanie but when people in Australia bang on about immigration they're not talking about nice white people coming from the UK or some other part of Europe. They're talking about Asians. It's racism wrapped up in what they call concern about immigration and even the ALP pander to that populist and mindless xenophobia. Neil Jenkins suffered racism all his life even from within his own family. That hurt like hell but none of them ever bothered. They couldn't have cared less'.

'You should come back home and stand for parliament yourself'.

'Home?'

'Australia?'

'This is my home now, Stephanie. Australia is just somewhere Neil Jenkins was born and brought up'.

They both ordered coffee to finish off their lunch and then Stephanie had to move things along. Stephanie prided herself on having a broad mind but even she would admit it was a little weird to have travelled all this way on the trail of a man only to be sitting here now with that man who'd changed his gender and looked like she'd got better legs than she had.

'Look, Elaine … '

' … I know what you want to ask me, Stephanie' said Elaine. 'It's like there's this gigantic elephant in the room, right? Well you know who I am. You know I used to be Neil Jenkins. You know that I came here and became Elaine Johnson. That's all of your initial questions answered'.

'Why the name Elaine Johnson?'

'Neil's Gran once told him that he would've been called Elaine if he'd been born a girl and Johnson was his Grans maiden name'.

'There's a lot more I need to ask you about, Elaine' said Stephanie.

'Let's walk back to the school' said Elaine. 'We can talk as we go'.

They didn't actually say much as they strolled back to the school. Then when they got to the gardens outside the main building Elaine stopped and asked Stephanie to sit with her on one of the benches. It was just inside the shade of a large tree which was welcome because the sun was blazing down. Stephanie explained to Elaine that it was Patricia who'd hired her to try and find Neil. Elaine burst out laughing.

'What's so funny?' asked Stephanie.

'Patricia' said Elaine. 'She's the most blatantly manipulative bitch Neil had ever come across. When he first discovered that Patricia was paying money to prostitutes through his account he was furious and when he confronted her about it she pulled at his heart strings and turned on the tears, pleading her case to him that she'd been desperate. But for Neil, it wasn't the nature of what the money was being spent on that was the problem. He was no prude and he wasn't naïve either. It was the fact that she'd done it without asking him and after having stolen his personal bank codes. That's what really got to him. Friends don't do something like that to one another. She was also trying to get her hands on the money he was getting from his father's estate. She wanted him to invest that money in the Ramberg corporation but he didn't want to. He wanted a project to invest in that was going to do some good somewhere and make a difference but Patricia was having none of it. That's when he really saw red. She'd been a good friend to him over the years but her way was to take over and if you didn't take her advice she'd get all defensive and emotional and that's when she was at her most dangerous'.

'She told me when she hired me that the two of you were on good terms when you left'.

'God, how can she be so ... the night before Neil left he had a blazing row with her and stormed out of her house'.

'She didn't describe it like that'.

'Well she wouldn't because it wouldn't fit with the story she was telling you'.

'You ... Neil took a hundred thousand of her money. She wants it back'.

'Well she'll have to whistle'.

'She won't like that'.

Elaine shrugged her shoulders. 'I can't help it. She can hardly claim the moral high ground when she'd hacked her way into Neil's account with money she was using to bribe people with sex'.

'You have a point'.

'And she didn't hire you because she was missing Neil' said Stephanie. 'It was only ever about the money'.

'Yes, I had worked that out' said Stephanie who thought they'd done an incredibly good job on Elaine's face. Sometimes a transsexual looked like ... well just a man in drag really. But Elaine's face had a real look of femininity to it and she a very feminine poise and what looked like, under her t-shirt, a nice looking pair of breasts.

'Neil went through hell at times, you know' said Elaine. 'He always felt like he was on the outside of everything, like his clothes didn't fit, his whole life didn't fit. He liked guys but nothing ever worked. He tried out the gay scene and went up to the bars on and around Oxford Street and the Cross so many times looking for something he never found. He had nothing against all the camp Queens but he didn't feel like he was part of that culture. There were one or two high times but they never lasted. He had a lot of sex with straight men who wanted to experiment but he just ended up feeling like an unpaid escort because they'd come round, tell him all their troubles, he'd show them a good time and then they'd be off again until the next time they fancied a bit of it. And it was always on the basis of they would contact him. He rarely had their number and didn't even know where they lived half the time. And when he fell in love it was always with a straight man. It was slowly killing his soul. It only came back to life when he made the decision to change into the woman he'd always felt like he was. He'd worked it out when he was a teenager. He didn't want a gay man's life. He wanted a straight woman's life. He couldn't go on living in a world full of men he couldn't have. He wanted to be able to look at a man in the street and not feel like he had to look away again as soon as he caught his eye. He wanted to be able to flirt openly with men without fear of either being ridiculed or beaten up. A couple of the straight men he fell for were big enough to say they were flattered by his feelings but that was all very well until he was alone in the still of the night with only a pillow to hold onto. He felt cold, isolated, alone. He found no comfort in anything. You've absolutely no idea how excruciatingly lonely it felt to be out of place within your own life. But there was a way to put it all right. There was a way for his true self to find the love he'd always so desperately needed. But it needed money and he'd only ever run to stand still financially. He had no savings. He'd spent his way out of misery'.

'I think I can get how he felt'.

'He thought he was going to end up going completely mad. He couldn't see his way out of the all the internal conflicts that were causing him such pain'.

'Couldn't his family have helped in any way at all?'

Elaine threw her head back and gave out a short laugh. 'His family wouldn't have given him the steam off their collective piss! He was the untidy mixed race element in an otherwise all white family and they were too ignorant to deal with it so they cut him adrift. They threw so many daggers in Neil's back and yet he was always there for them, you know? But you see, they're the sort who never say sorry and never make amends. It always has to come from the other person in any dispute because they have to be able to say that the other person came crawling. They're pathetic. Weak, spineless, stupid, and pathetic and yet they believe themselves to be so strong. They couldn't lose face. They were lost in their own feeble little worlds. But Neil's genes were from something different and they couldn't handle a boy who didn't look exactly like them because his father had come from a country called Syria'.

'My father was hard to get along with, Elaine, God rest his soul'.

'Did you manage to work around it?'

'Most of the time we did' said Stephanie, recalling all those moments with her father when it felt like they were always butting heads. 'He died a couple of years ago'.

'I'm sorry'.

'It's okay'.

'At least you had him for all those years though. Neil never even had a glimpse of his father'.

Stephanie didn't quite know what to say to that. Although she'd locked horns with her father many times over the years she still loved the old goat and she always knew that he loved her. That put her at a distinct advantage to Neil and she understood that. You don't always appreciate what you've got until you meet someone who's never had it. And people who say you don't miss what you never had are talking shit when it comes to a missing mother or father. Stephanie had learned that much from her experiences.

'Neil's family life wasn't the best but I guess he at least had his friends'.

'Oh he had some bloody good friends and he had a good social life' said Elaine. 'The family he'd chosen rather than the family he'd been stuck with were the best'.

'And what about your life now, Elaine? Has it all been worth it?'

Elaine smiled brightly. 'Oh yes. His name is Hans. He's German and every time I look at him I have absolutely no doubt that it was all worth it'.

Stephanie couldn't help smiling back at Elaine's face. She looked like a teenager who was experiencing her first crush. 'Is he here?'

'Yes, he's working in his office upstairs in our flat. He's a freelance journalist and he came out here from Berlin to do a story on this place. He ended up staying and he's based himself here now'.

'And he's what you always wanted?'

'And more' said Elaine. 'I know it's going to sound like some ridiculous cliché but he makes me feel like I've always wanted to feel and I'm lucky, Stephanie'.

'I'm pleased for you, Elaine'.

'Thanks. I went through a lot to get there but I'm there now. I'll introduce you later'.

'You'd better'.

'But look, you want to know about that night, don't you?'

'The police have issued a warrant for Neil. They suspect him of Mariam's murder'.

'I thought they would'.

'So did Neil kill her?'

Elaine's face contorted into pain and anguish. 'Neil adored his half-sister Mariam, Stephanie. He couldn't believe it when she made contact. When they met it felt so perfect and so beautiful. She was his sister and she'd come half way round the world to try and make things up to him. She acknowledged that her family had done him wrong. She said sorry. That's all he needed. They talked and talked and Neil told her about the operation he wanted to have and she supported it. She said he should use some of the money their father had left him. He only knew her a short time but he absolutely adored her. They were so close. No, Stephanie, he didn't kill her'.

'But what did happen that night, Elaine?'

Elaine started to cry. 'Patricia Palmer killed Mariam'.

'What?'

'And that's the real reason why she'll never get one bloody cent of her hundred thousand back!'

.

Stephanie was more than a little surprised by what Elaine had blurted out. 'Elaine, are you really saying to me that Patricia Palmer killed your half-sister Mariam and then buried her in a shallow grave?'

Elaine didn't answer. Her tears were running down her cheeks but she was making no sound.

'Elaine? You can't seriously be saying that Patricia Palmer is capable of something like that?'

'You already know what she did with Neil's bank account'.

'But it's a pretty big leap from that to murder?'

'A hundred thousand dollars is a lot to spend on sex'.

'But it still doesn't point to her being capable of murder'.

'She's capable of anything if the need arises' said Elaine. 'Look, she's manipulative and she'd make you believe that Florence Nightingale was a serial killer if it suited her purposes. She's good and she can't help herself'.

'Elaine, she was your friend'.

'She was Neil's friend' said Elaine. 'She's no friend of mine'.

'Elaine, I know this is painful for you but I can only help you if you tell me exactly what happened that night'.

Elaine wiped her face with her hand. 'Patricia was the only one who knew about the short cut through the woods that Neil always took when he drove up to Palm Beach. He'd driven her up there with him and taken that route several times. In that last row he had with Patricia he'd told her that he was taking Mariam up there for the weekend. She was the only one who knew of his plans, Stephanie. She tipped them off'.

'Tipped who off, Elaine?'

Elaine didn't answer.

'It was your other half-brother Touma al-Ashwari, wasn't it?' said Stephanie.

Elaine looked at her. 'How did you work that one out?'

'Well what's puzzled me all along is why the hospital in Zurich where Mariam worked had never tried to find out what had happened to her. But more to the point, why had none of her family tried to find out? That bit really didn't make sense. It must've been because someone had told them what had happened and that could only have been the murderer. I sat one day and put two and two together. Then I rang Achi'.

'You spoke to him?'

'He was pretty hostile'.

'I'm not surprised' said Elaine. 'Hostility is his style. He's dangerous, Stephanie. Don't mess with him'.

'I understand. But let's get back to the night in question'.

'Neil turned the corner and a figure stood in the middle of the road holding up a gun at the car like they were expecting the car to come round that corner. That's why I'm convinced

Patricia tipped her off. Anyway, Mariam screamed and Neil slammed on the brakes. It was

particularly dark round there what with all the trees and it was hard to make out any

distinguishing features but the figure looked like a man who was dressed in black right down

to a black hat, black gloves, a black scarf hiding half of his face. For a moment or two

nobody moved. It was like the three of us were frozen in time. Then Mariam said out loud

that it was our brother Touma. Neil told her to stay in the car but she said she had to try and

reason with Touma so she got out before he could stop her. For a few seconds they shouted at

each other and then he shot her. Neil got out and ran round to her but it was too late. Her eyes

were wide open. She'd gone. There was blood pouring out of her neck. The bullet must've hit

her carotid artery. He cried out with the pain of the incredible loss that was overwhelming

him. He felt so utterly helpless. He'd have given anything in that moment to bring her back

but he knew it was no good. Then he heard Touma coming closer and thought it was all over

for him too.

'Touma, I'm your brother!' Neil pleaded.

'No infidel is a brother of mine!' Touma shot back.

Neil started to panic breathe. Touma pointed the gun straight at him but it when he pulled

the trigger the barrel stuck. The gun had failed to shoot. Touma was frantically fiddling about

with it and trying to make it work. Sheer terror was running through Neil. He didn't know if

Touma had another gun or a knife or some other weapon that he'd lunge at him with. But

then it struck Neil that this was his chance to get away and so he got to his feet and ran as fast

as he could. He thought Touma would come after him and after a few meters he dared to look

behind him. He wasn't being followed. He carried on running. He was crying with sorrow,

the deepest, deepest sorrow that poor Mariam was dead. The world had stopped spinning. It

had gone crazy'.

'So what did he do then?'

'He came across a bus shelter on the main road but of course nothing was going to be stopping there until the morning. So he found a spot in the bushes behind the shelter and hid himself away until the sun came up. Then he got on the first bus that came through and headed back into the city. None of the other passengers on the bus took any real notice of him. Most of them were still half asleep as they contemplated the day at work ahead. Neil's head was all over the place. He wanted to go back and see what had happened to Mariam's body but he was too scared. He felt guilty about having left her like that but what else could he do? He just had to get away'.

'He left the country on that day?'

'Yes. Once the bus had got him into the city that morning he bought some new clothes and booked himself on a flight to Singapore that afternoon. He sneaked back to his flat to collect his passport and then he was gone'.

'Why didn't he just go to his friends and tell them what had happened?'

'Because he was terrified of putting them at risk. If Touma came after him then one of them could've got hurt. He didn't want to be near anybody he cared about for that reason'.

'And did Neil make the decision then to come to Chomburi?'

'It seemed to make sense' said Elaine. 'Neil checked the news reports and nothing had yet been reported. No questions were being asked about anything. Either they hadn't found the car yet or they were putting the details together of what they had found before releasing it to the public. It was bloody painful in terms of leaving everybody behind but this was his chance to get away. At times in those first few weeks he missed his friends so much it was like a physical pain and he wondered if he'd done the right thing. But he knew deep down that he had. The day he checked himself in to the clinic was the day he said goodbye to being Neil Jenkins and began the process of becoming Elaine Johnson'.

'It didn't make the news bulletins until the next morning' said Stephanie. 'I've checked'.

'Neil was given time' said Elaine. 'Someone was helping him somewhere in the universe'.

'All his friends were desperately worried, Elaine'.

'Please don't try and lay a guilt trip on me, Stephanie'.

'I'm not trying to do that, Elaine. I'm just telling you that people like Alan Ford and Andy Green still miss Neil and still worry about what happened to him. They'd be so relieved to know that Neil ended up okay'.

'I am planning to go back' said Elaine. 'I want to explain. I want them to understand what I did and why'.

'So after killing Mariam and trying to kill you Touma must've somehow got back to Switzerland' said Stephanie. 'A false passport?'

'I can't think of any other way he could've done it' said Elaine. 'Touma is an extremist. He belongs to a group that's using the civil war in Syria to try and bring about an Islamic state based on Sharia law. Mariam and my father believed in a secular, open, democratic state where everyone's individual human rights are respected. That's what caused all the conflict in the family according to Mariam although it hadn't always been like that. They'd all been secularists but Touma had attended a mosque in Zurich that was known for its radicalism. That's where he was turned according to Mariam. Added to that was Neil's existence which

Touma came to believe brought shame on the family. All of that mixed together was like an incendiary device in Touma's soul. I was an infidel and Mariam was as good as for supporting me'.

Stephanie sat back. She was almost exhausted. 'But Elaine, you surely can't believe that Patricia was somehow in league with Touma?'

'No, of course I don't believe that' said Elaine. 'But I do think that it was Patricia who tipped him off though'.

'She might not have had any choice given that Touma was planning murder. He might've threatened her with all sorts'.

'No, I know. But all she had to tell him was where they were going and then maybe call the police or call Neil to warn him. That's what I find unforgivable'.

'Elaine, I have to ask, have you had any contact with the authorities since Neil left Australia?'

'About three months after I checked into the clinic I transferred some money to the group in Syria that Mariam and my father supported. I thought it was the right thing to do. Anyway that led to me getting a visit from the Australian security services. Two of them turned up here one day'.

'Here in Chonburi?'

'Oh yes. I'd started surgery and I was lying in bed' said Elaine. 'They told me that using official government sources they'd traced Neil's money and found me here'.

'So they've known where you were and what you were doing for almost the entire time?'

'Oh yes' said Elaine.

'Well it doesn't look like they talked to their colleagues in the police'.

'I can't answer for that' said Elaine. 'All I can say is that I told them everything I knew and they said that Touma had been watched by the Swiss authorities for several years but that he now spent most of his time in Syria. Well how do you apply an extradition warrant from a country that's in the middle of a very bloody civil war?'

'You've been through a lot, Elaine'.

'Yes, but deep down inside I'm happy now, I'm content and I'm at peace with life'.

'I hear Beryl Hamilton was trying to find you?'

'Yes, but we pretended she'd got hold of the wrong end of the stick. She never actually got to meet me before we were able to throw her off the scent'.

'Do you know what she wanted?'

'To use me in some kind of feud against Patricia' said Elaine. 'But I didn't want any part of that. I have enough of my own bones to pick with Patricia and I didn't want to join in some daft feud between those two women that goes back years. So I stayed hidden as far as she was concerned. But look, I'm exhausted with talking for now and besides, here's a reason to take a break'.

Stephanie followed the path of Elaine's eyes and saw a tall man in his mid-thirties walking towards them. 'Is this Hans?'

'Yes, this is the man who makes me feel on top of the world'.

Stephanie was rather taken with Hans too. Apart from being tall he had broad shoulders, dark blond hair that was beginning to go thin a little on top, blue-grey eyes and plenty of stubble on his face. The sleeves of his light blue shirt were rolled up to his elbows and his faded blue jeans went down to a pair of brown leather sandals. He was rugged and sexy. The top couple of buttons on his shirt were open exposing a chest rug. His smile opened up his entire face as he stepped closer to Elaine and they kissed. It was serious kissing and Stephanie cleared her throat to remind them that she was there.

'Sorry' said Elaine.

'It's great to meet you' said Hans in a deep, German-accented voice and shaking Stephanie's hand. 'Are you staying over tonight? We could maybe all have dinner?'

'Oh please say you will' said Elaine.

'Alright' said Stephanie, smiling. The two of them looked so happy together. 'I'd love to. But is there a place here where I can plug in my laptop? I've got a whole lot more to put into the file on this case. And I'd like to see more of the school if that's okay?'

'We'll take you on a guided tour' said Elaine. 'After we've had some tea. I'm gasping after all that talking'.

'Just one thing, Elaine?'

'Yeah?'

'You told me why you didn't let Beryl Hamilton connect with you. So why did you let me?'

'My friends Colin and Michael thought it would be a good idea'.

'Colin and Michael?'

'Colin Turner and Michael Benson. They're a couple. Colin is a pilot for Qantas and Michael is a consultant surgeon. Michael used to live at Fiona Thompson House and they kept in touch with Andy Green which is how I met them. Colin's connection to it all is that he was a friend of Andy's going way back and he's also the step-son of one of Patricia's ex-husbands, a guy called Stephen Morrell'.

Stephanie looked up to the Heavens. 'Patricia, Patricia, bloody Patricia. I'm sure I'm going to find out next that she's connected to the royal family in some way'.

'She has got her fingers in a lot of pies for sure' said Elaine. 'Anyway, Colin and Michael have been the only friends I've kept in touch with. They've been here to visit and whenever Colin is on a Bangkok stopover he comes here. I swore them to secrecy, even to poor Andy, because I just didn't want word getting out'.

'But why them and not Andy or one of your other friends?'

'You remember I said that Neil caught a flight from Sydney to Singapore on the day he disappeared?'

'Yes?'

'Well it turned out that Colin was the Captain on that flight and when he did his PR walkabout of the cabins as Captains do, he of course saw Neil. Neil went back with Colin to his crew hotel in Singapore and over a few beers he told him everything about what had happened to Mariam and what Neil was planning to do'.

'So they've known all along?'

'Yes'.

'You asked them to keep some pretty big secrets, Elaine'.

'I know and I owe them dearly for it' Elaine admitted. 'But I knew I could trust them'.

'So how does this get to me?'

'Colin and Michael thought it would be interesting to see who'd hired you although we did kind of have a good idea'.

'You guessed it was Patricia?'

'Yes. And the guess was educated by years of knowing the woman'.

FIONA THOMPSON THIRTEEN

Stephanie walked through the door that exited customs and into the arrivals hall of Sydney airport. This time Wayne was standing there waiting and she rushed into his arms.

'Pleased to see me?' he asked.

Stephanie looked up at him and smiled. 'What do you think?'

They kissed in that way that new lovers do when they've been apart for a few days. Then Wayne said 'Well you can go away more often if you're going to come back and be like this'.

'I've missed you'.

'I've missed you too, Miss Marshall'.

'No prostitutes this time?'

'None whatsover'.

'Well I'd love nothing more than to go back to your place or mine and celebrate being back together again'.

'But?'

'I've got some serious work to do, Wayne, starting with Patricia and David Palmer. But I'm going to finish early, say about four? Then you can have me all evening and all night'.

'That sounds good to me'.

'You'd better knock one out this morning though so you're not too desperate tonight'.

Wayne laughed at Stephanie's suggestion although on second thoughts it might not be such a bad idea. He had been unbelievably horny whilst she'd been away and he didn't want to reach the finishing line too early later on. 'You're so dirty'.

'Isn't that one of the reasons you like me?'

'One of them' said Wayne who then kissed Stephanie again, slowly and with passion. 'I've so missed the taste of you'.

'You can show me how much later'.

'I take it things got a little complicated over there?'

'Yes but it wasn't all bad news'.

'You did find Neil Jenkins?'

'Yes' said Stephanie, cautiously. She'd made an agreement with Elaine that she could tell people who she was and that she was planning on returning to Australia.

'But he's now Elaine Johnson?'

'Yes. Come on, I'll tell you all about it in the car'.

Wayne dropped Stephanie off at her office and then went off to work. She opened up and dealt with the mail whilst she waited for Patricia to meet her there at her appointed time of nine o'clock.

'Well I hope you've got some good news for me' said Patricia, firmly. 'You've been racking up a rather large bill across South East Asia'.

'Oh I think you'll want to know what I've found out, Patricia' said Stephanie. 'But let me start with a question for you. Did you tell Touma al-Ashwari where he might find Neil Jenkins and Mariam al-Ashwari on the night Neil disappeared?'

Patricia struggled to speak and maintain her composure but then she couldn't help capitulating. 'Yes is the simple answer to that' she said.

'I see'.

'Could I sit down, please?'

'Be my guest'.

The weather outside was dull and grey and moisture was hanging heavily in the early summer air. It matched the atmosphere inside where the two women were squaring up to each other. No wonder Patricia didn't have many friends, thought Stephanie. She was a total nightmare. And these little incidents where she starts off challenging then backs down like a child in the face of Stephanie's refusal to pander to her nonsense were starting to wear just a little bit thin.

'I don't usually open the door to people unless I know who it is' said Patricia, her best tortured face back on again. 'When you have money and a certain position in life you can't be too careful. There's always someone wanting to grab it all off you. So I always check a caller's ID before I open the door unless, as I said, I already know them. But that day Touma al-Alswari managed to get into the building when someone was going out. He came straight up to the apartment and because it was a knock on my actual door I thought it must be one of the neighbours. So I opened it and that's when it all began'.

'All what began?'

'He pulled a gun on me' said Patricia. 'He wanted to know everything about my friendship with Neil and asked me if I'd met his sister Mariam. I said that I hadn't met Mariam. He said he didn't believe me. He grabbed hold of me and pushed the gun under my chin. Stephanie, I was terrified. I told him my husband would be back any minute but it didn't seem to deter him in any way. Then he told me to sit down and he produced an envelope. He told me to look inside. It had everything to do with my family in it. Pictures of my twins John and Angela, my grandchildren, David's son Robert. They were all there along with addresses and pictures of where they all lived. Touma threatened to kill them all one by one unless I told him where she could find Neil and Mariam. I'd already had the row with Neil and I wasn't in a good place emotionally, added to that I had this man in the apartment who was threatening to kill me and everyone in my family. He said he'd start with David when he got home'.

Patricia broke down and started crying. Stephanie couldn't help sitting beside her and placing a consoling arm around her shoulder.

'It must've been pretty frightening'.

'I didn't think I was going to survive the day or even the next hour'.

'How did he find you, Patricia?' asked Stephanie. She'd kind of had enough of Patricia always claiming to be the wounded party when the truth was that it was Patricia's own scheming that led to many of her downfalls. She just didn't seem to know when to leave well alone.

'Neil told me that his half-sister had contacted him and had come down here to Australia to see him' Patricia revealed. 'I lied before but I had good reason'.

Stephanie sighed. 'And I'll be glad to hear it. Go on'.

'I contacted the al-Ashwari's in Zurich' said Patricia.

'You did what?'

'I wanted one of them to come down here and cause some trouble'.

'Well you got your bloody wish!'

'But I never imagined he'd cause the kind of trouble that would lead to Mariam's death, Stephanie, I swear! I just wanted to persuade the al-Ashwari's to give over control of Neil's inheritance to me in a trust so that he wouldn't spend it on anything that might disgrace the family as they called it. Yes, I was playing on their traditions as Muslims … '

' … for your own ends! You were colluding with an extremist. And from what you say do I take it you told Touma that Neil was planning to have trans gender surgery?'

'Yes'.

'So that was another lie you told me, Patricia. You said you didn't know what he was planning'.

'I never agreed that he had to do all that to himself to be happy. I thought he just needed to meet the right guy and that it just hadn't happened yet but when it did he'd be alright'.

'You had no business going behind his back like that'.

'I was trying to be a good friend'.

'You were trying to get your hands on his money! At least be honest about it, Patricia, just for once'.

'Alright, alright, you can put me in the gutter if you want to' Patricia retorted, fighting back. 'But I was there all those times when Neil thought he couldn't face the future and he was contemplating doing away with himself. I was there and talked him into surviving. I was there when he felt like life was totally against him and I brought him back from the brink. So don't you dare, don't you dare lecture me on anything'.

'Oh I'm sorry but it's a bit different being there for your friend when he's down and trying to take steps to make a smash and grab on his money! I mean, what were you going to do with Neil's half a million? Were you really going to let it sit in a trust find gathering interest for when he met the right guy and he could start living at last? Of course you weren't. You were going to use it to invest in Rambergs and all your other businesses'.

'I would've built him a really decent portfolio'.

'You would've used his money to shore up your own finances!'

'But I would've been helping him at the same time!'

'Yeah, sure'.

'Oh you think what you like, frankly, I really don't care'.

'And all your meddling led to a woman being murdered by her own brother and Neil only escaping with his life because the gun caught when Touma tried to murder him too'.

'So that's what happened?'

'Yes, that's what happened. Neil managed to run away and decided that was his moment to finally take control of his life and go through with the surgery'.

'Is he … is she okay?'

'She's very happy, Patricia. She did the right thing'.

'I'm really sorry about Mariam, I truly am and again, if you don't believe that, I don't care but it's true. And I'd have never forgiven myself if anything had happened to Neil'.

'So Touma al-Ashwari came to see you because you'd contacted him?'

'Yes' Patricia admitted. 'I thought we could do business and nobody would get physically hurt. But I was wrong. When I heard Touma talking to me on the phone with all her extremist language I panicked and told her the deal was off. That's when she turned up at the apartment'.

'So you told him where to find them and you even spelled out the route that Neil would take'.

'I didn't think I had any choice!'

'You could've warned Neil!'

'I thought that if I did that then Touma would come back for me or carry out his threat against David or one of the other members of the family' Patricia pleaded. 'I've lived with that for three years'.

'Yes, well Mariam hasn't lived with it because she'd dead'.

'And I'm sorry and I mean it. What's her name now?'

'Elaine Johnson'.

'And is she planning to come back to Australia?'

'Yes' said Stephanie. 'She is planning to come back'.

Patricia was glad to hear that. She did want to try and make it up with her old friend whether anybody believed her or not.

'The police may want to talk to you, Patricia'.

'The police?'

'It could be argued that you were an accessory to murder' Stephanie pointed out.

'Are you going to tell them?'

'Well I'm not going to go knocking on their door' said Stephanie. 'But if they come knocking on mine then I'll have no choice'.

'Well I have more immediate concerns relating to who is desperate enough to try and destroy my business interests that they made a false allegation about me to the tax authorities'.

'It was Beryl Hamilton' Stephanie revealed. She didn't think there was much point in maintaining confidentiality with David. Patricia would find out soon enough. 'She also came after Neil Jenkins'.

'Why?'

'Because she wanted to use him against you' said Stephanie. 'Elaine dismissed the idea of being in contact with Beryl because Beryl's reasoning was that she wanted to get Neil in a fight against you'.

'Well, well, well' said Patricia who relished the thought of putting on her boxing gloves again for a fight with little Miss Hausfrau. There's no feud like an old feud. 'So Beryl has been trying to bring me down'.

'You know her of old I understand?'

'Oh yes' said Patricia with a grin she couldn't help. 'You could say that. She's always has been a vindictive cow and she's never forgiven me for the fact that David chose me over her even though it goes back years and she's now worth millions more than I am'.

'Well she does seem to have it on for you'.

'No change there then' said Patricia. 'So bring it on if Beryl Hamilton wants a fight because she'll get one. Looks like the old days are back'.

David Palmer flew down to Melbourne and took a taxi round to see Beryl. He would have to calm down by the time he got to her house. He was incandescent with rage over his ex-wife's treachery against Patricia. It was a million years since he and Beryl had written their place in history and life had moved on for them both. Why did she have to go picking at old wounds now?

Beryl lived in the affluent West Melbourne suburb of Williamstown and it struck David how different it all was from when he and Beryl were together thirty years ago. The detached mansion in its own grounds and with a swimming pool was a far cry from the bungalow semi they'd had in Albert Park when they were bringing up John, Susan, and Kevin. Robert had been born there too but David had never had any hand in his upbringing. David had been a truckie, driving up and down the country to support his young family. David and Beryl were young too but they'd never gone in much for a social life outside the home. David had been content to come home to his family, a beer or two in front of the telly and Beryl's pavlova. It was only when life's twists and turns brought Patricia back into his life that he realised how much of him had been dead. Not that he'd ever wanted to take anything away from Beryl. She'd been a good mother to the kids, especially John who, although he wasn't hers she'd treated him like he was and absolutely no differently to Susan and Kevin. She'd been a good wife too and kept a good home but it was Patricia who'd lit the fire in his soul all those years ago when they were kids and that would never change. Even though she'd left him, even though she'd taken the baby Angela and left him with the baby John, even after all those years had passed, David had never stopped loving Patricia. And that was still the case. Beryl had gone through one or two relationships since she and David had split up but eventually she'd settled with Gordon Hamilton, Wayne's father, Patricia's ex-husband, and the tangled web of the lives of the Palmers and the Hamiltons were forever linked in children, but more importantly in jealousy, spite, and memories that just wouldn't let go.

'David' said Beryl after she'd opened the door and led him inside. 'It's nice to see you'.

'Nice place you've got here'.

'Well it's handy for Bob to get to and from work at Tullamarine. Did you fly down here on Air Australia?'

'No, I didn't. I came on Qantas'.

'Oh I see. That's loyalty for you'.

'Don't you even dare, Beryl' said David who was struck by how little Beryl had really changed over the years. The face made her look a little older but the hair was still set and curly albeit it looked like it was seen to by a more expensive stylist these days.

'I take it from your tone that this isn't a social call'.

'You're damn right it's not'.

Beryl stared at him for a second. 'My God' she said. 'You look just like your father used to do when he came to see us at Albert Park. Remember? Standing there like that with your hat in your hand. And it was normally because he thought we should be in trouble over something'.

'He'd turn in his grave now'.

'David, do you mind telling me what I'm supposed to have done?'

'Oh here we go' David sneered. 'Ever the perfect Beryl. Butter wouldn't melt and everyone's husband is safe because of her morals and her standards. What a joke. What a bloody hypocrite'.

'Look David if all you're going to do is walk in here and insult me then you know where the door is'.

'Why did you try and do Patricia in to the tax authorities?'

'Who says I did?'

'Oh come on Beryl you've never been a good liar so don't bother starting now'.

'No, that's right. I left all the lying to you and Patricia because it's what you were both so bloody good at!'

'Unbelievable. All these years and you still can't take your claws out of Patricia'.

'She deserves to have something bad happen to her, David, God knows she's done enough in her time to warrant something coming back at her. But do you want to know why I did it? Do you want to know why I tried to cause trouble for her?'

'That's what I've come down here for'.

'Because she gave a home and a job to Wayne, that's why. And in case you'd forgotten he murdered our daughter!'

'It was Andy Green who gave the home and the job to Wayne and it was against Patricia's better judgment if you must know'.

'Easy for you to say now'.

'But wait a minute? You've had nearly three years to start mixing it?'

'I wanted to wait a decent time after Gordon died'.

'What? Before you slipped into Bob Sanders bed?'

Beryl slapped David's face.

'Well now' said David. 'A man speaks the truth to a woman and she doesn't like it so she assaults him. Women have been getting away with that for centuries, Beryl, just like you've been getting away with this holier than thou image. Well it's tarnished now, Beryl. You're tarnished. Your halo slipped and it's got mud all over it. And it's all been for nothing. Yes, true enough, life got a bit uncomfortable for Pat financially for a while and she'll need to take certain steps to recover things fully. But the tax people have finally accepted that the reason she was behind with her returns was because her accountant hadn't been paying them and she knew nothing about that. Curiously enough, he's now shot through. So tell me, Beryl? Tell me how long it took you to set it all up?'

'I don't know what you're talking about'.

'No lies, Beryl!' David demanded. 'We know it was you who shopped Patricia and we know you went looking for Neil Jenkins to ask him to join you in some pathetic vendetta against her. So it was you, wasn't it? It was you who paid the accountant to stop paying out Patricia's taxes and it was you who gave him a nice little golden handshake to disappear. Wasn't it? I said wasn't it?'

'Yes, it was! And I'd do it over and over again to avenge Susan's murder'.

'Do you not think I feel sick to the stomach every time I look at Wayne? Every time I see him breathing? Do you not think that Susan goes through my mind every single day and I wonder what she'd be doing now if she hadn't been killed? You haven't got the monopoly on pain, Beryl. But Wayne has done his time and I have to respect that otherwise there's no point in having a justice system. It doesn't make it alright. It just makes it bearable'.

'For you maybe' said Beryl. 'Never for me'.

'Well alright, if that's how you want to look at it. But I'm warning you, Beryl. If you come after Pat like that again then so help me you'll regret it because every time you hit her you hit me as well. Life is treating you well again, Beryl. I hear you're getting together with Bob Sanders and that's a good thing so don't spoil it with all this nonsense. Don't be the small minded little house mouse you've always been. This time take control and grow up. You never know. It might suit you'.

'How could I ever have loved you, David?'

'I think the same thing about you every time I look at Patricia'.

Elaine Johnson liked her breasts. No, that wouldn't be enough of a superlative. Elaine Johnson loved her breasts. They weren't enormous but they were enough for Hans to make a meal out of licking them and sucking on her tits, brushing his short beard against her skin gently as his chin went between them. This was her most erogenous zone and he'd get so carried away that she'd be bursting with pleasure and arousal.

She loved to lie down underneath him and open her legs so he could work his way inside. He'd get into his rhythm and she'd feel the tip of his cock against the sensitivity of her prostate. This was how she enjoyed the sensation of full sex. When they'd first got together he'd been gentle with her and he'd been very aware of her potential limitations sexually. But she hadn't come all that far just to settle for being only half a woman and she'd been assured by the clinic that she should be able to enjoy the pleasures of normal sexual intercourse that would be equally as enjoyable for the man she was with too. It would feel to them both like it would for any man and woman and for Elaine it wasn't so much that Hans was physically inside her. It was the psychological penetration that was worth all the pain she'd gone through and made her cry out with joy and pleasure. Hans knew everything about her past as Neil Jenkins and it didn't bother him in the least. He said that he'd fallen in love with the woman who was Elaine Johnson and the past didn't matter to him at all. She was also good at giving him oral satisfaction which was a knack he appreciated and one that she'd brought with her from when she was Neil Jenkins. He'd always known how to pleasure a man well in that way.

She was lying in Hans' arms without a care in the world after they'd made love. He kissed the top of her head.

'What are you thinking about, darling?' he asked.

To hear his deep voice call her darling made her feel so special it was like hearing a voice from another world. Nobody had ever used romantic terms of endearment to Neil Jenkins. No man had ever made him feel complete like Hans made her feel complete. If only for that she knew she'd done the right thing to make the change.

'I'm thinking that I don't know which feeling I like best' said Elaine. 'The feeling of excited anticipation before we have sex or the feeling of absolute contentment once we've had it'.

'I just like it all' he said, squeezing her tight.

'You're so romantic'.

'That's because you're so beautiful'.

'We never really talk about the future, Hans'.

'What about the future? It is ours. That's that'.

'Well for obvious reasons I can't have children'.

'Well then we can adopt' said Hans.

'As simple as that?'

'Why not as simple as that? We are together, we are in love, we can't make our own children so we adopt a couple of kids who really need us. We're surrounded by them here'.

'It wouldn't bother you not to have your own kids?'

'No' said Hans. 'I don't have this big male ego thing of needing to pass on the family line. Besides, even though I'm the oldest I have two brothers who I'm sure will be doing that before too long. And working here has given me a sense for all kids out there who are in desperate need and we could provide for them. To be honest, I think that's doing a better thing for the human race than having your own kids which at the end of the day is a quite selfish act, you know? It's quite egotistical. Better to give your love to a couple of kids who are already here and in need'.

'You make the most perfect sense'.

'Don't I always, liebling?'

Elaine raised her head and kissed him before settling back down again with the side of her face in the fur on his chest. 'Always, darling'.

'I had this Aunt and Uncle who couldn't have kids. The problem was with my Uncle apparently who had a very low sperm count. Anyway, they tried and tried and my Aunt became obsessed, you know? She wouldn't hear anything about adoption. It had to be her own kid and she would literally order my Uncle home from work when she was most fertile. She became so obsessed with it all that she ended up ditching my Uncle and taking off with another guy who got her pregnant within a couple of months. Because that's what it was all about, you see? My Aunt wanted her own child and she didn't really care who she had it with. It broke my Uncle's heart once he realised that he wasn't enough for her. But she didn't care about that either'.

'How is he now?'

'He's with another lady now. She has two grown up children, they live in Dresden and they're very happy'.

'I like a happy ending'.

'Speaking of which, are you nervous about next week?'

'You mean about going back to Australia?'

'Ja'.

'My own little happy ending?'

'That's the one'.

Elaine had received a message from the Australian embassy in Bangkok that the new passport she'd applied for was ready for her to go and collect. That meant that she and Hans could fly down to Sydney as soon as they were able to make definite plans. It wouldn't be quite as simple as that to collect her passport of course. The message said that she'd need to show them an almighty long list of 'required' paperwork to prove who she was now and who she'd been before.

'Well yes, I'm nervous' Elaine admitted. 'I'm nervous about all sorts of things to do with it to be honest'.

'What?' Andy Green exclaimed after Patricia had dropped her bombshell. 'You're selling Fiona Thompson House?'

The tax authorities had now ended their investigation into Patricia's affairs following an admission from Beryl Hamilton that she'd tipped them off without good reason. They said that in any case they'd not been able to back up the claims with any real evidence although the whereabouts of Patricia's accountant was still a mystery. They also said that they couldn't find any evidence to back up Patricia's claim that Beryl had paid her accountant off just to cause trouble. But Patricia had now asked Stephanie Marshall to find her accountant. And when she did Beryl had better brace herself because Patricia would unleash Hell on her.

'This is my most valuable property, Andy and I've got a lot of back taxes to pay' Patricia reasoned. 'If I manage to get the asking price I should be able to pay them all off'.

'So you do it again'.

'Do what again?'

'Come up smelling of roses' said Andy. 'I might be out of a job and a home but you'll still be wrapped up in dollars every night'.

'Andy, I don't want to have to do this. But it's either this or go bankrupt and what choice out of those two would you make?'

'Yes, Patricia, I know. But the prospect of unemployment isn't very exciting, especially when I've got Maddy's wedding next year'.

'Andy, when did I say your job was at risk? I've still got all the other properties, you idiot. Your job is safe. You just might not be able to carry on living here'.

'And that goes for Wayne too?'

'Of course' said Patricia. 'But his job is safe too and for the same reasons as yours is'.

'I hear Beryl Hamilton is none too pleased about Wayne being here?'

'You heard right' said Patricia. 'But the day I concern myself with the likes of what she thinks is the day I curl up and die. We both know that I didn't like the idea of you giving Wayne a job and a home but David convinced me it was the right thing to do and he's got far more reason to see Wayne in the gutter than I have'.

'David's always been a decent bloke'.

'Too decent for me you mean?'

'Patricia, I didn't say that'.

Patricia smiled. 'Oh don't worry I'm only teasing. Anyway, back to this place. I've already got a pair of potential buyers and they're very interested. When I tell you their names you might not be so worried that they're going to throw you out on the streets'.

'Well who are they?'

'Well you knew one of them from way back in the day' said Patricia. 'He moved to New Zealand with his family after his mother married my ex-husband Stephen Morrell. The other one was living here around the time Susan was … was killed. Then he moved on and whatnot. Anyway, they're a couple now and they want to buy this place'.

'You don't mean Colin Turner and Michael Benson?' asked Andy, his mood lifting at the thought of two of his friends buying the house.

'The very same' Patricia confirmed. 'Now do you really think that two of your oldest friends would see you out on the streets?'

Elaine and Hans arrived in Sydney and were picked up by Michael Benson who brought them to stay at his and Colin's house in Double Bay, one of Sydney's eastern suburbs and not far from the Pacific coast. It was a very modern house just a stone's throw from the beach and was surrounded by trees inside a high dark green painted wooden fence. The boys were big fans of very modern art and they had several pieces around the place. They were also into Asian art whether it was wooden carved heads of Buddha from India or the delicate minimalism of Japanese pottery, the boys had pieces of it displayed everywhere. Elaine loved their place. Their tastes were so similar to her own.

Hans decided to lounge by Colin and Michael's pool in the back garden whilst Elaine went to see her mother. She reckoned it might get messy between them and she didn't want Hans to have to go through that even though he was more than willing. This was a meeting she had to effect on her own. Stephanie Marshall picked her up and drove her out to her mother's house and on the way Elaine told Stephanie about the questioning she'd had to undergo from the police when she'd arrived back in Australia. After they'd accepted that Neil wasn't the murderer of Mariam al-Ashwari, they'd gone down another line of investigation.

'They seemed to think that I might know where Touma is' said Elaine. 'But he tried to kill me. Why would I know where the mad murdering bastard is?'

'Why don't they know where he is?'

'Well apparently, the Swiss authorities have him down as having caught a flight from Zurich to Beirut in Lebanon last month. They decided to monitor him instead of trying to detain him because they thought that by doing that it might prove to be more useful overall'.

'Even though he's wanted for murder by the Australian authorities?'

'Yes' said Elaine. 'But it's all part of a joint intelligence thing being carried out by several countries who are trying to see just who are the bad guys and who are the good guys in the ongoing conflict in Syria. They think Touma might lead them to people who can give them a much clearer picture than they have already of what exactly is going on'.

'Meanwhile, the apprehension of Touma for the murder of your sister Mariam comes a very poor second to strategic the interests of world powers?'

'That's about it, yes' said Elaine. 'But look, I do get it. The conflict has to stop. You've seen it all on TV? Too many innocent lives are being slaughtered and Touma could lead them to some very valuable information about people who they might be able to negotiate with'.

'That's a very generous way for you to look at it'.

'I think Mariam and probably my father would've looked at it the same way' said Elaine. 'But anyway they lost Touma in Beirut and now they haven't got a bloody clue where he is'.

'So their plan badly backfired?'

'So far, yes'.

'Do you think he might be heading out here?'

'When he's wanted on a murder charge? That would be a bit audacious even for him. Anyway, he had a lot more opportunity to get at me in Thailand. Out here would be far more difficult for him'.

'He's done it before, Elaine'.

'Yes, but like I say, he didn't have a murder charge on his head then' said Elaine.

'No' said Stephanie. 'He was just your average extremist bent on killing his sister and half-brother because they'd dared to defy his extremism'.

Elaine laughed. 'Well putting it that way … I shouldn't joke about it but I have to at times'.

'Laughing in the face of adversity is often the best way of dealing with it'.

'You're right there' said Elaine. 'I've never been able to get my head round how different Mariam was from Touma. They really were like chalk and cheese'.

'It happens in families' said Stephanie.

'To be honest, Stephanie, I'm more concerned right now with this conversation I've got to have with my mother. It's going to be one of the most difficult I've ever had. I feel sick to be honest with you'.

Stephanie pulled up outside Connie Weston's house and Elaine got out. She stood straight and stole herself. She looked good in her dark blue dress with thick straps across her shoulders and a hem halfway up her upper legs. She'd quite taken to wearing shawls to complete her outfits and today she had a black and silver one draped round her shoulders. Stevie Nicks had always worn shawls and she'd always loved the way Stevie looked.

When Connie Weston opened the door there was a moment when she genuinely didn't recognize who was standing there in front of her. Then the penny dropped and the colour drained away from her face.

'Do you want to give me a bloody heart attack?'

'Oh so as usual it's all about you, Mum'.

'I don't have a daughter' Connie snarled.

'You do now' said Elaine. 'And look, I turned out pretty good'.

'Why didn't you tell me you were coming?'

'So you could arrange to be out when I got here? Neil had enough of that when he was growing up and living at Grandma's and I'm certainly not going to let you abuse me in that way or any other. What's the matter, Mum? Cat got your tongue? Not used to any of your kids standing up for themselves?'

'You'd better come in' said Connie. 'You've got some explaining to do'.

'Oh no' said Elaine, firmly. 'I don't have any explaining to do as you put it and if you're only letting me in on that basis then you can forget it'.

'Just bloody come in, will you? If you don't want to explain then at least be willing to give me some answers'.

'Okay' said Elaine. 'Then on that basis I will come in'.

Connie walked through to the living room and slumped down on the sofa. She poured herself a scotch from the bottle on the small table next to it and offered one to Elaine who accepted and took a large swig from it. She could feel it burning as it went down her throat. Last night Colin and Michael had cooked dinner for her and Hans, Andy Green, and Stephanie and Wayne. They'd managed to down eleven bottles of wine between them, plus some champagne before hand and a couple of glasses of brandy afterwards. It had been a great night but one which Elaine's head was remembering more than the rest of her. But she needed the scotch. It was a necessary slap of Dutch courage. Despite her bravado she couldn't remember ever feeling more nervous.

'Just tell me why' said Connie.

'I always knew I'd been born into the wrong gender'.

'Oh stone the flaming crows this isn't morning bloody telly!'

Elaine stood up. 'Right, that's it. I'm going'.

'Sit down!'

'Don't speak to me like that!'

'I said sit down!'

'And I said don't speak to me like that!'

Connie stood and squared up to her. 'You're not too bloody big or too bloody clever to get one across your face for talking to me like that'.

'Oh so you can talk to me like I'm a piece of shit but it doesn't work the other way?'

'I'm your mother!'

'No, you're not. You're just some woman who gave birth to Neil. Grandma brought him up, not you'.

Connie raised her arm to slap Elaine's face but Elaine was too quick for her and grabbed her wrist in mid air. 'You hit me once and so help me I'll unleash over thirty years of pent up anger and hatred against you with my fists. And I don't think you'd survive that'.

The two women sat down again and there was a pause whilst a very heavy silence fell on the room.

'You really do hate me that much?' asked Connie.

'Yes' said Elaine. 'I really do hate you that much'.

'Then why are you bloody well here?'

'Because despite everything I thought you might be worried or concerned about what had happened to Neil and I wanted to put your mind at rest'.

'Put my mind at rest? That's the most absurd thing anybody has ever said to me. Put my mind at rest when you turn up like this?'

'Like what, Mum?'

'Like some bloody circus clown that's what'.

Elaine swallowed deeply. 'Still the same old pig ignorant bitch you ever were'.

'Oh so because I'd expected my son to remain my son and not become my bloody daughter you think that makes me a pig ignorant bitch, do you? Well I wear the badge with bloody honour!'

'No it doesn't make you a pig ignorant bitch, Mum, because you always were one'.

'Your Grandma will be turning in her grave'.

'Don't try and lay that on me because Grandma would've understood. How she bred someone like you I'll never know'.

'And how I bred a freak like you I don't know so that makes us quits'.

'Oh I know how you bred me. You opened your legs for a man who was far more interesting than you and then your poor little brain with its total lack of intellect just couldn't keep up'.

'I reckon they get the surprise of their bloody life when you open your legs'.

'Why would they? I'm a woman now in every way including sexually. They inverted Neil's penis to make my vagina'.

Connie pulled a disgusted face. 'Christ, I don't want to know'.

'No. You always did have a problem with the truth, didn't you Mum? Like when you denied that my father had ever given you any money for me when really he'd given you a lump sum to invest. And you did invest it. In your wedding to your racist husband who forced you to abandon me and you invested some of it in this house'.

'I was owed that money'.

'It was my money, Mum!'

'I deserved it more!'

'But it wasn't yours!'

'Well its history now so get over it!'

Elaine smiled. She was so going to enjoy this. 'Well I could always turn nasty and ask the courts to make the decision. You see, I've got all the documents from my father's side of things saying he intended the money to be placed in a trust fund for me. I could force the sale of this house to finally get the cash that's owed to me but that would put you and your pig ignorant racist husband out on the streets'.

'You wouldn't do that to your own mother?'

'You wouldn't ditch your own son because your husband wouldn't accept him because he was mixed race?'

'I don't believe you'd be able to prove it'.

'Oh yes I would. In fact my lawyer says I've got a cast iron case because the documents my father prepared make it very clear. So how do you think it would feel, Mum? How do you think it would feel to be kicked out on the streets at your age?'

'You haven't got the nerve'.

'I've got the nerve and I've got the legal back up'.

'So what are you going to do?'

'You're going to gift me the house and I'm going to rent it back to you'.

'Are you out of your bloody mind? This is our retirement nest egg. All our money is tied up in this'.

'No, Mum, all my money is tied up in this. You wouldn't have been able to buy this house if you hadn't stolen money from me, the money that was meant to give me the kind of start in life that you'd never be capable of. And you stole it. You stole it from me'.

'I can't believe you're so bitter'.

Elaine threw her head back and laughed. 'Bitter? You made it clear time after time that Neil wasn't to consider himself part of you or your new family. Then you had the bloody nerve to stop my father from contacting me even when you'd rejected me out of your life. Bitter doesn't even begin to cover it'.

Connie was dismissive. 'Oh you were always playing that bloody sob story record'

'It's the truth. Neil lived it and I'll carry it with me the rest of my days'.

'You don't know who the fuck you are. I should've sent you for treatment years ago'.

'What, and made me into someone you could handle rather than the real person I was? Classic behaviour of parents who aren't particularly bright or educated'.

'Christ, you really have got it in for me, haven't you?' said Connie as a wall of emotion was beginning to fall on her. 'The kicks in the teeth just keep on coming'.

'Well I learned from someone who did it to her son Neil countless times without any thought for his feelings. He grew up with emotions that were shattered and broken because of you'.

'You've been waiting for this'.

'Yes, I have. I've been waiting for the chance to turn the tables on you'.

'But I'm your mother. Doesn't that mean anything to you?'

'Did it mean anything to you that Neil was your son?'

'I should've had an abortion when that Arab bastard made me pregnant'.

'No, Mum' said Elaine. 'You should've had me and then dropped dead because that way you would've done us both some good'.

'You really hate me, don't you?'

'Yes, Mum, I really do'.

'The feeling's mutual'.

'The fact that you hated Neil was clear right from the start but you see, Neil tried to love you. You just wouldn't let him. Well I'll never try to love you, Mum, because I know it just isn't there as far as you're concerned and I'm not going to go down a one way street for years like Neil did'.

'Well I think you've said enough and I'd like you to go now, please'.

'You've said a lot too, Mum, but as usual, that's erased from history so you can blame me for everything'.

'See yourself out'.

'My lawyers will be in touch regarding the house. Don't even think about fighting it or making any trouble. I've got much more cash at my disposal than you'll ever have. I can hire the best. You can't'.

'We'll see what your father has to say about that'.

'My father is dead, Mum. But if you mean that narrow minded racist scum bag you're married to then I'd advise him to accept my plans without question if he knows what's good for him'.

Connie wouldn't look at Elaine. 'I think I said to see yourself out'.

'It didn't have to be like this, Mum. If you could only open your heart and grow your tiny mind then we could reconcile'.

'Just go, please'.

'Didn't think so' said Elaine. 'Well it's your loss in every respect'.

When Elaine got back into Stephanie's car she couldn't hold it back any longer and burst into tears.

'I take it that didn't go well?' said Stephanie.

'Stephanie, I've just turned into Patricia Palmer. Please drive us to the nearest pub. I need a bloody drink'.

FIONA THOMPSON SIXTEEN

Colin Turner and Michael Benson pulled up outside Fiona Thompson House and got out of their car. They leaned against it for a moment or two just to look up at what they'd bought. Although they were both stalwart members of the ALP and believed in a fairer more egalitarian society, they also knew that they had to do something with the money they made.

'This is where we first met, remember?' said Colin.

'How could I forget?' answered Michael, smiling at the memory. 'You'd just moved back from New Zealand to start your pilot training out at Kingsford Smith and this was the only place you knew to see if you could find somewhere to live'.

'And you were in that ground floor flat'.

'Just waiting for life to come along and happen'.

'Then I walked through the door'.

When Colin and Michael met nobody in their immediate circle of family and friends knew that either of them was gay. Colin had once come out to Caroline Morrell and her daughter Samantha but he'd never told his mother or his step-father Stephen. Michael hadn't fully come to terms with himself at that point let alone spoken about his feelings to anybody else. But as soon as he saw Colin he knew that the wondering was over. If there was one for him then Colin was it. When they started talking and it became clear that Colin thought the same about Michael they decided to go for dinner together that night. Colin moved into Michael's flat the next day and they've been together ever since. And when they did come out to their respective families both sides said they'd guessed as much years ago and it had never been a problem for any of them since.

'It'll be twenty five years next year'.

'I know. We still haven't decided what we're going to do for it'.

'Celebrate the fact that we're one of the few couples we know, gay or straight, who've been together that long and are still as happy as we ever were'.

'Well said Captain Turner'.

'We're two of the lucky ones Doctor Benson'.

'I reckon I must have something to have kept you away from all those cute flight attendants who'll do anything for four stripes and a Captain's salary'.

'Lucky for you then that I do handsome rather than cute' said Colin. 'Anyway, what about all those male nurses who are always out to bag a doctor?'

'Lucky for you then that I do handsome rather than cute' said Michael as they both laughed. 'I wish I could kiss you now'.

'Careful' said Colin. 'This is Australia where the first woman Prime Minister was against gay marriage. This is not like when we were in London and could get away with showing a bit of affection in public'.

'I know. Who'd have thought it? The old colonial power racing ahead of us at galloping speed on gay rights'.

'Well unless you're suggesting we move all the way over there to be part of what's going on I think we'd better stick to campaigning here. But in the meantime we'd better go and check out our investment. Andy will be waiting for us'.

'I wish Fiona herself was here' said Michael. 'She made this place. She was such a good person'.

'But she also had her more fierce side too, Mike' said Colin. 'Remember what she was like with Andy when he was bringing Maddy up? She was always on his back about something. You know as well as I do that she could be a complete cow to him at times'.

'Yeah, but she meant well' said Michael. 'She always did 'I miss her anyway'.

'Oh I miss her too' said Colin. 'Don't get me wrong. She was a character and no mistake. I just don't think she was always the angel you seem to think she was. For saying she was once a prostitute she could be incredibly judgmental. She had her flaws like we all do and if you weren't in her good books then you knew about it'.

'I suppose we forget when someone dies that they weren't always a perfect human being'.

'Who is?'

Patricia drove round to Colin and Michael's house to see Elaine. She knew the boys were out because she was due to meet them at Fiona Thompson House but she had to see Elaine first. She turned up unannounced and although she'd known what to expect, still the sight of Elaine, a woman who used to be her friend Neil, made her pause and widen her eyes.

'It's rude to stare' said Elaine as she stood at the front door. 'Didn't anybody ever tell you?'

'I haven't come to fight' said Patricia. 'It was just a bit of a shock seeing you like that'.

'Well don't get used to it because you won't be seeing much of me' said Elaine.

'There's no need to be so damn hostile! I was going out of my mind with worry about you when you disappeared, so was David, so was everyone else so don't jump on your bloody high horse because if you've got things to say to me then I've got one of two things to throw back on behalf of all the people you left without a bye or leave'.

'I suppose you have a point' said Elaine. 'Come in'.

Hans was in the shower. He and Elaine had been having a sleep in that morning to flush all the remains of the jet lag out of them. It also gave them the chance to indulge in some rather wicked and wonderful sex. Elaine had then taken first turn at getting ready because she took longer and therefore the ever Germanic ways of dear Hans had worked it out that she should always take first turns in the bathroom. She was more than ready for Patricia and whatever the duplicitous cow had to say.

'I hope you weren't expecting a red carpet' said Elaine.

'I don't blame you if you're unsure of me' said Patricia.

'That's big of you'.

'Look, I realise you've been through a lot. It must've taken a lot of guts to do what you did and for that you have my upmost respect'.

Elaine laughed sardonically. 'Your attempt at sincerity is funnier than watching the latest stand- up comedian'.

'Look, you've got to give me the chance to explain' said Patricia, her voice bleating with a silent request for sympathy. 'I never meant to hurt … I never meant to hurt Neil'.

'But you did!' Elaine threw back. 'He trusted you. He thought you were there for him. But the only place you really wanted to be was with his money'.

'That's not true'.

'Don't tell me it's not true because we both know that it is! Look, Patricia, Neil opened up his heart to you in a way he'd never done with anybody else. He told you how sad and lonely he'd felt all the way through his childhood and how he felt trapped in a life he didn't understand. And you took advantage of that for your own ends'.

'I wouldn't do that, Elaine'

'Yes, you would. You'd do it in a heartbeat if it suited you'.

'I explained everything to Stephanie Marshall and … '

' … yes, I've heard it all, Patricia. I've heard how the police have let you off from being prosecuted for conspiracy to murder because you told them all about Touma. I know all about Jill O'Donnell and what you were trying to do for the Ramberg corporation. I've heard about the financial difficulties you could've been in if Ramberg's had got into serious trouble and that's why you wanted to use my money to cushion yourself. I've heard it all, Patricia'.

'Then you'll be able to understand how desperate I was'.

Elaine scoffed. 'You've got some hope, lady. And why didn't you ring and warn Neil that night that Touma was coming after him and Mariam?'

'Because I was scared' Patricia insisted. 'I was scared of what she'd do to me or a member of the family if I'd warned Neil. Look, Elaine, I want us to try and get back to the way we were before. I've missed … I've missed you'.

'I think it's better if you leave' said Elaine. 'You're out of my life, Patricia. It was sometimes nice knowing you'.

'Just remember who was always there for you when you really needed someone'.

'I will. Just like I'll always remember who it was who used my account to launder money'.

'I thought you might've tried to understand' said Patricia who was becoming increasingly angry with the holier than thou attitude Elaine was putting on. 'I admit I did some things that I shouldn't have and for that I truly am sorry. But I won't be used as a rag for you to wipe your conscience on. We were friends. We were good friends'

'Then you went and ripped all that apart!'

'Because I was desperate!'

'You know what, Patricia? I don't care. My life is now about Hans and me. You can go and do whatever the fuck you like'.

Patricia stepped up close to Elaine. 'I'm not going to waste anymore of my time but do you know what? I used to be someone who was feared. Then I settled down and became a respectable businesswoman. Well now the events of the last few weeks have forced me back into type. Watch yourself. I don't take prisoners'.

'Don't you threaten me'.

'Oh I'm not threatening you, Elaine. I'm telling you that it wouldn't do you any good to cross me. I just wanted to warn you. For old times' sake'.

'I'm deeply moved by your concern. Now get lost'.

Undeterred by the chill of her meeting with Elaine, the next call Patricia made was on Wayne.

'What the hell do you want?' Wayne wanted to know.

'I think we can dispense with the usual polite formalities' said Patricia. She brushed past him and into the flat. 'We need to talk'.

'Come in why don't you?'

Wayne followed Patricia into the living room. 'I realise that I'm the last person you'd ever want to talk to'.

'You got that right' said Wayne. 'Now I know you own this place but I'm a tenant and I do have rights'.

'I don't own it anymore. I've just sold it. Try and keep up'.

'Oh that's right. You've had to sell this place to pay off all the taxes you tried to swindle out of the government'.

'My accountant was paid to withhold those taxes. I wasn't responsible'.

'That's what you always used to say when you'd caused a whole heap of trouble'.

'Wayne if you'd just give me a chance you'd learn that I'm actually here to help you'.

Wayne sat down on the sofa and outstretched his arms along the back. 'Go on. You may as well after you so politely let yourself in'.

Patricia sat in the armchair. 'The reason why my accountant almost brought about the financial ruin of me is because he was being paid by somebody to do it'.

'Yes, I know, it was Beryl'.

'Doesn't Stephanie keep anything about her clients' cases private?'

'We have a relationship of trust' said Wayne. 'Has David managed that with you yet after all these years?'

'Don't try and be funny' said Patricia. 'It really doesn't suit you'.

'Say what you need to say, Patricia and then go'.

'Why does everybody treat me like I'm the evil one when it's me who's been wronged here?'

'Look, Patricia, I know the whole story where Elaine Johnson is concerned'.

'Oh yes and I'd forgotten you were Mr. Clean these days'.

'What do you want? You see, I've got rooms where I could be watching paint dry'.

'Alright, I'll get to the point. I want to help you get what's rightfully yours'.

'I beg your pardon? You want to help me?'

'You're entitled to millions of dollars worth of shares in Air Australia, Wayne. You know it, I know it, David knows it, everybody knows it, including and especially the people who would stop you from getting it'.

'Beryl and Robert Hamilton'.

'Your step-mother and step-brother. It would be no skin off their nose for you to get what's yours. They'd still be rolling in it'.

'I'm not interested, Patricia'.

'Don't give me that, Wayne'.

'Look, I've got a job, a place to live, and I've met the most wonderful woman in Stephanie. That's all I need, Patricia. I'm not interested in claiming any money from Beryl and Robert because money brought me nothing but trouble in the past and I don't want to go back to those days. Now I know why you're doing this. You want to use me to cause trouble for Beryl. Well I'm past all that. I don't want anything to do with it'. He stood up. 'I'd like you to leave now, please'.

Patricia stood up too. 'You know me, Wayne. When I want to achieve something I stop at nothing to make it happen. And nobody knows your old self like I do. Nobody knows how to get to that old self and remind him that he wasn't always unsuccessful in getting what he wanted and that with me on his side the idea of failure just wouldn't come into it. Think of all that money, Wayne. Think of your absolute entitlement to it. Think of what you could do with it. You could invest it wisely and set you and Stephanie up for life. You don't need to get back into the old game. You just have to dip your toes in the water to get what's yours'.

'Please, Patricia. I'm a different person now living in a very different place'.

'I'll give you time. Air Australia is expanding fast and its stock value is going up all the time. Think about it. I'll see myself out. See you at the party'.

A drinks party had been organized in the garden of Fiona Thompson House for all the residents of each of the nine flats there. Not all the residents had been able to make it. Two had previous work commitments and one was inter- state, but it was a chance for those who were there to get to know their new landlords, Colin and Michael over a glass or two of Australian sparkling wine. As she stood holding hands with Wayne, Stephanie counted around a dozen people including Patricia and David who were making the introductions. Then Andy walked up to them.

'Well look at you two' said Andy. 'Love's young dream'.

'I don't know about young' said Stephanie.

'But you can call it a dream come true' said Wayne who then looked at Stephanie and they kissed.

'Oh puh-lease, get a room'.

'We have one' said Wayne. 'Just behind you and when we feel like it we'll retreat there'.

'Enough information, thank you!' said Andy. 'But no, it's good to see the two of you like this'.

'Thanks, Andy' said Stephanie.

'Yeah, thanks mate' said Wayne. 'So when are you going to get yourself a piece of the action?'

'One of these days' said Andy who was becoming increasingly unconvinced that he'd ever meet 'the one'. 'Or maybe not'.

'I never thought it would happen to me, Andy' said Wayne. 'Not in a million years'.

'Well, we'll see' said Andy.

'Colin and Michael look like they're good people' said Stephanie.

'Yeah, they are good blokes and I think they'll be good landlords too' said Andy. 'Colin hasn't really changed much since I knew him before and to be honest, it's good that I'm going to see less of Patricia from now on'.

'We'll all drink to that' said Wayne who was keeping as far away from Patricia as possible. She was right. He was entitled to millions. But it was the cost of all that money in the way it can pollute and pervert even the most well intentioned of people that was making him shy away from her most generous offer of assistance. It was just what he didn't want. Not now his life was beginning to come together in a way that had never felt so good. He couldn't go down the old road again. He just couldn't. He'd got a taste of life and love in a simple way and he wasn't going to risk that for all the money in the world.

'What was it that Patricia wanted when she called round this afternoon, Wayne?' asked Stephanie. 'I saw her coming out of your place when I got here'.

'She wants me to claim my share of Air Australia from Beryl and Robert and she says she'll help me do it'.

'And her reason is?' Andy questioned knowingly.

'She wants to cause trouble for Beryl as a way of getting back at her for all the trouble she caused for her with her accountant'.

'I've found her accountant by the way' said Stephanie. 'My associate in Singapore, a guy called Kevin Lee, has discovered him practicing there. I've passed the details onto Patricia'.

'God help the accountant' said Andy.

'I think she's in the right on this one though, Andy' said Stephanie. 'He did try to get her into strife in return for cash from Beryl Hamilton'.

'You three look very serious huddled together like this' said Patricia after stepping up to them. 'Not talking about me, I hope?'

'No, Patricia' said Wayne. 'We were talking about someone who's interesting'.

Patricia threw her head back and gave out a chortle. 'Oh the old ones are always the best. Listen, Stephanie, what with everything that's been going on I didn't thank you for the great job you did for me. The result wasn't quite as I'd expected but you sorted that out and you sorted the question of who was trying to ruin me. I authorized the bank transfer to pay your final bill today. It should be in your account in the morning'.

'Thanks, Patricia. It's been a challenging case not least because you lied to me right from the start'.

Patricia looked uncomfortable. 'Yes, well I had my reasons'.

Stephanie then looked up at Wayne. 'But there have been some rather nice compensations'.

'Yes' said Patricia, looking at Stephanie and Wayne smiling and deciding to knock the ball straight back. 'Has he told you about his marriage to Karen Fox and how she ended up dead?' She read their expressions. 'No, I can see that he hasn't. Well I hope it doesn't spoil the party for you. I'd watch myself if I was you though, Stephanie. Most of the women Wayne gets involved with end up dead in some way'.

'Patricia, that was vintage you and totally uncalled for' said Andy.

'But I think that Stephanie should know everything' said Patricia, innocently. 'And I speak as her friend'.

'Oh you're really taking us all back now' said Andy. 'How many times did I witness you sticking the knife in and making it look like you were handing someone a cup cake'.

Patricia smiled. 'Yes it's a skill I've cultivated over many years'.

Stephanie was raging. If she was the kind of woman who thumped people then Patricia would be decked right now. There were probably a thousand things in Wayne's past that he hadn't told her about. It goes with the territory of being with a man with his kind of history. But it didn't matter to Stephanie. She really couldn't care less. What mattered to her was the man she loved now and when he wanted to reveal everything he would. She could feel Wayne's hand sweating and his fingers tighten around hers.

'You're right, Patricia' said Stephanie. 'Wayne hasn't told me about this Karen Fox but can I warn you to keep your nasty tongue to yourself? I'm with Wayne now and if you want to get to him so you can use him as a puppet on your particular string then you'll have to get through me first and believe me, I don't take kindly to playing games with a woman who thinks she's superior to me because believe me she isn't. Wayne will have his own reasons for not telling me about Karen Fox and I trust him. Now I can do that because I'm not you with your clear sense of paranoia. Enjoy the rest of the afternoon'.

To say that Patricia was sent away with a flea in her ear would be an exaggeration but she looked sheepish as she went to rejoin her husband David and forget about how she'd failed to have the last word with Stephanie and Wayne.

'Wow' said Andy. 'I wish you'd been around a few years ago, Stephanie. You'd have put her in her place when she was in her absolute prime and no mistake'.

'Too bloody right' said Wayne. 'I will tell you about Karen Fox later. I won't leave anything out'.

'I know' said Stephanie. She was desperate to know now but this wasn't the time or the place. 'But let's talk about something else'.

'Like the cricket for instance, Miss Marshall?' Andy teased.

Stephanie threw her head back. 'No, anything but the bloody cricket!'

'Now why would that be?'

'Because all you'll do is rub my bloody nose in it about England's performance in the first Ashes test'.

'Well that's a tough one' said Andy who was laughing with Wayne. 'I mean, your compatriots gave us Aussies plenty of wriggle room to have a go'.

'Alright, enough!' said Stephanie who was laughing now too. 'We'll get you back. Don't get smug'.

Maddy walked up and took advantage of Wayne talking with Andy to Colin and Michael to take Stephanie to one side. 'Can I talk to you for a minute?'

'Sure' said Stephanie. 'What's on your mind?'

'First of all, you've got to agree that you didn't hear this from me and what I'm about to tell you is regarded as classified?'

'Well you've got me intrigued but yes, of course I agree' said Stephanie. 'I wouldn't drop you in it, Maddy'.

'No, I know but I had to make sure' said Maddy. 'Look, it seems that there are more irregularities in the original report into Neil's disappearance. There's going to be an official enquiry but it looks like somebody pulled some information from that original report'.

'And how do you know this now?'

'Because it's suddenly reappeared' said Maddy. 'That's the weird thing about it all. It's just suddenly reappeared. It was never in there before'.

'And it's to do with the footprints?'

'Yes'.

'Well we know that they didn't check on the driver's side otherwise they'd have found the prints belonging to Mariam al-Ashwari'.

'Yes, but the file that has conveniently found its way back into the main case notes says that there was also two other sets of footprints, one of which we assume belonged to Touma al-Ashwari and the other … '

Maddy didn't get a chance to complete her sentence. She was shot in the back and fell forward into Stephanie's arms, blood pouring out of her shoulder and her eyes wide with shock and terror.

FIONA THOMPSON SEVENTEEN

Everybody threw themselves to the ground. They were panicked but frozen with terror at the same time. Attacks like this don't happen in good old Aussie suburbs like Manly. This was one of the centers of hedonism in the greater Sydney conurbation. This was where people came to have fun and seek out a relaxed lifestyle. This wasn't where people expected someone with a gun to go on the rampage in the middle of a sunny afternoon.

'Everybody inside now!'

Slowly they each raised their heads and saw Touma al-Ashwari pointing a shotgun at the assembled crowd. The few seconds of stunned silence gave way to cries for help for poor Maddy who was lying there wounded. Andy had lifted her head and was holding her in his arms. Wayne and Stephanie were holding her hand.

'What the hell do you want?' Michael demanded. 'I'm a doctor. Let me see to Maddy'.

'Shut your perverted mouth!' roared Touma. 'Or you'll die. Now get inside. Everybody! I won't tell you again'.

'My daughter needs an ambulance' said Andy, frantically.

'Then she's not in luck' Touma retorted. 'If any of you try and make a call I will kill you'.

Andy stood his ground. 'I said my daughter needs an ambulance and she needs it now!'

'Look, I just want to help her' Michael repeated. 'You've got to let me'.

'Do you think I care if she dies?'

'Come on, Touma' said Elaine. 'Let Michael help and let someone call for that ambulance'.

'You're all going to die unless they do as I say'.

'For God's sake, the girl needs help!' pleaded Wayne. 'Now I don't know what it is you want, mate, but it can't be about letting this girl lie here without medical attention'.

'He's right' said Michael. 'You're doing yourself no favours like this'.

'Surely you know you can't succeed with something like this' said Colin. 'Somebody will have heard the shots and called the police. They'll be here any minute'.

'How pitifully you infidels plead for your God forsaken lives' snarled Touma.

'Alright, that's enough!' said Elaine. She stood up. Hans stood up with here and told her to get back down here but she placed her hand on his arm and smiled. She said she'd be alright. 'Maddy has nothing to do with why you're here and we both know that. In fact, let everyone else go and you and I can talk. Because it's me you're here for. The rest of the people here have got nothing to do with our private business'.

'Our private business?' Touma questioned. 'You make it sound so … reasonable'.

'It can be reasonable if you let it' Elaine pleaded. 'But what good are you doing with all this? Now put the gun down and we can talk but these people have nothing to do with it'.

'My daughter needs a bloody ambulance!' Andy cried out. 'For God's sake she's slipping away here!'

Stephanie and Wayne were trying to help Andy see to Maddy but Andy was growing ever more distraught. Patricia and David were huddled together, frightened out of their lives and realising just how old they were getting. There was a time when David would've leapt up and dealt with Touma but he couldn't move that quickly anymore. Meanwhile seconds were beginning to feel like minutes and nobody knew what to do. But Colin was beginning to formulate a plan. His training as an airline pilot included how to handle siege and hijack situations. But this wasn't a classroom setup. This was real life and lives were at risk.

'And I told you she was out of luck!' Touma repeated.

Andy then lost it. He stood up and moved towards Touma who fired a single shot at point blank range straight into Andy's chest. Blood and parts of his insides flew across the garden and everyone was either yelling at Touma or screaming.

'Oh what's the matter, infidels?' Touma goaded. 'Can't stand the sight of blood and death? Well it's what you've been putting my people through for years!'

'My people?' Elaine scoffed. 'My people? You're Syrian, Touma. Your people have been engaging with the West for decades. The President's wife is British, remember? Your people are your extremist group with their twisted vision of Islam. The greater population don't want Assad but they don't want people like you and your group either and do you know why? Because they want to be able to send their daughters to school. They want to be able to walk down the street and hold hands with their loved one if they want to. They don't want women to be forced into covering themselves up. They want everyone to be equal and everyone, men and women to be free. They want to be able to do simple things like listen to music and go to the cinema with their Christian and Jewish friends. And yes, if they feel like it they want to be able to have a drink of an evening. And if you don't know that then you haven't been listening. But then your group doesn't listen, does it, Touma? You just tell people that they want your version of Islam and kill them if they disagree. Everybody is your enemy if they don't agree with you one hundred percent. Well when I read the Koran it said nothing about the shooting of an innocent man and his daughter being the gateway to paradise. It's not what Allah would support you doing'.

'Don't you dare say the blessed prophet's name!'

'Oh save it! Somebody got into your head. You're not a crusader for the soul of the Islamic faith. You're a criminal. You're an extremist. And you're a murderer who shot his own sister. I think that Allah is waiting but not with open arms'.

'You know nothing!'

'I know that there's a father and daughter here who are in urgent need of medical help and you're not letting them get it!'

'A good father wouldn't let his daughter dress in a short skirt like that'.

'And do you really think that Allah is bothered about that? Right now when they're both fighting for their life? You really are a stupid bastard'.

'You won't speak with such fake courage with my bullet inside you'.

'Well you've tried to kill me before. Come back to finish the job? Well go ahead if it makes you feel any better'.

'Elaine!' Hans called out.

'It's alright, Hans, darling. You just stay back there and stay still'.

'You are the poison in the blood of our family'.

'Really? Well no, Touma, you're the poison because Mariam was a decent person, our father by all accounts was a decent person and your mother thought it right that Neil should get what he was entitled to which makes her a decent person too. But you, you're the odd one out because you're a murderer who's jumped on a religious bandwagon for cover. Now do one decent thing and let somebody call for that ambulance and at least you'll have that to tell Allah about when the time comes'.

'I told you all to get inside!'

'I think we'd better do what he says, Michael' said Colin, trying to calm everyone. He knew what he was going to do. He just had to get Touma inside. He was slight. He'd be easy to overpower once they got him with nowhere to escape to. It shouldn't be difficult. 'Come on, everybody. Let's get inside'.

Everybody started moving indoors. They were terrified but a flash of recognition passed from Colin to Michael and then to Hans, Wayne, David and some of the others there.

In the hallway of the house Touma ordered everybody to keep moving down inside. Stephanie could see that Patricia was visibly shaking. She hadn't expected her to react like that. She thought she'd have done everything she could to get control of the situation back from Touma but what she was more concerned about was poor Andy and Maddy and what the hell was going to happen next to bring an end to this nightmare.

She didn't have to wait long to find out. Hans lunged at Touma in a sideways movement that saw him grab him from behind and place his hands firmly on the shotgun, forcing Touma to lift it up and point it at the ceiling. Colin, Michael, and Wayne joined Hans and in a matter of seconds they'd wrestled the gun from Touma in a blaze of hysterical condemnations that Touma was screaming out as he continued to struggle. Stephanie then took the scarf she'd been wearing and used it to tie Touma's hands behind his back then they pushed him onto his stomach and Hans held the shotgun at the back of his head whilst David finally made the call to the emergency services and Michael ran outside to see what he could do for Andy and Maddy before the ambulance arrived.

'Do you know how to use that?' asked Elaine, looking at the shotgun Hans was now holding.

Hans winked at her. 'Army training back in Germany. I know exactly what to do with it if necessary'.

'Would somebody please explain what the hell is going on here?' Patricia pleaded.

Michael then came running back in. 'Maddy is still alive' he said, softly before rubbing the back of his neck and shaking his head. 'But Andy … well I think you all probably know from the way he was shot at such close range. He's dead. I'm sorry'.

Touma al-Ashwari was arrested and charged with the murder of Andy Green and the attempted murder of Maddy Green. Elaine was briefed by the Australian security services. It seems that Touma had intended to use his hostages at Fiona Thompson House to bargain for the release of two prisoners held in Australian jails who were members of the same extremist group as Touma and who were being held on suspicion of planning terrorist attacks in Australia. He further confessed that he'd been planning to shoot a hostage every twelve hours until his comrades had been released, starting with his half-sister Elaine who had been the reason he'd been drawn back to Australia and this particular mission.

After they'd gone Elaine broke down and wept for what felt like hours in Hans' arms.

Patricia made it known that she was intending to sue the security services for what she called 'negligence' in letting someone like Touma al-Ashwari enter the country, even though he'd come in on a false passport. She was warned that there was no hope in her pursuing the case but she was determined nonetheless. Somebody had to pay. Somebody always had to pay as far as Patricia was concerned.

'My fiancé Ralph has been fantastic' said Maddy who was resting in the flat she'd shared with Ralph for several months now. 'The boys, Colin and Michael, have been great too. Michael drops in every day and Colin has offered to take me on one of his working trips to Los Angeles to do some pre-wedding shopping'.

'Really?' said Stephanie who'd come to visit. 'Are you going to go?'

'Well I think I might' said Maddy. 'I know he'd look after me and since he's gay Ralph has got no reason to worry'.

Stephanie laughed. 'No, that's true. He and Michael have not had a very good start to their new ownership of Fiona Thompson House'.

'No, but I think they're dealing with it. None of the residents have decided to leave after what happened. They recognize that it had nothing to do with the house itself'.

'Well that's something'.

'I was really pleased to see Elaine the other day after Dad's funeral' said Maddy. 'I'm glad she came to see me before she and Hans headed off'.

Elaine had decided to go back to Thailand with Hans and for them to live their life there for now. There'd been so much tragedy since she'd arrived back in Australia that she couldn't bear to risk anymore if she stayed. She said she'd stay in touch with everyone, that they'd all be welcome to visit them in Chonburi, and that when she and Hans decided to get married they'd all, except for Patricia and David, be invited.

'Yes, I'm going to miss her' said Stephanie. 'I've grown to rather like her'.

'Yeah, me too' said Maddy. 'She's another one who's been wrapping a supportive arm around me these past few days. She blames herself for what happened to Dad but I made it clear that I don't blame her. It wasn't her fault that her half-brother had turned into an extremist. And I can see so much of Neil in her, you know? If that doesn't sound too weird?'

'No, I mean I didn't know Neil of course but I think I can guess what you mean' said Stephanie.

'And I feel sad for her' Maddy went on. 'I mean, she lost her Dad without even having known him. Then she loses her sister and now her brother who wanted to kill her too will be inside for a long time in a very high profile way. Then there was everything to do with her gender identity. She's been through a lot'.

'I know' said Stephanie. 'It doesn't seem fair. But look, how are you doing?'

'Well they're taking some of my stitches out tomorrow'.

'I didn't mean that, Maddy'.

'I know you didn't' said Maddy feeling that all too familiar lump in her throat. She was battling with an almost overwhelming sense of loss. She'd had to live without her mother all her life and now her beloved father had been taken from her in the weeks before her wedding.

She was finding it a real struggle to get over what she saw as the unfairness of it and the injustice. Her father had been there for her every step of the way when there was nobody else around and now he wasn't going to be around to see his grandchildren. It just didn't seem fair. She was putting on a brave face but in truth she was screaming inside. 'But it's a hard question to answer'.

'I know but look, Wayne and I aren't going anywhere. I know we're not your Dad but we'll be here for you'.

'That's one thing I am pleased about' said Maddy. 'It's just … every day is a mountain to climb, you know. Sometimes its okay then other times it's like I can't put one foot in front of the other'.

'It's only been a few days' said Stephanie, holding Maddy's hand. 'You've got to give yourself time, love'.

'Easier said and all that'.

'Well at least now the funeral is out of the way' said Stephanie. 'That's the hardest part, believe me'.

'I know but … I just can't bear the thought that I'll never see him again, you know? I can't bear the thought that I'll never be able to ring him up for a chat and know that he's there just like he's always been. I miss his physical presense in my life. It's hard, Stephanie. It's so fucking hard and it's so fucking unfair that I've lost him'.

Stephanie held Maddy whilst she sobbed. She was close to tears herself. Her heart really went out to Maddy. The poor girl was suffering so much pain and none of it was of her own making.

'I'm sorry' said Maddy once she'd regained her composure.

'Don't say sorry' said Stephanie. 'You've nothing to be sorry for'.

'I don't think I'll ever get over losing Dad. I think I'll come to terms with it at some point in the future and I'll accept it. But I'll never get over it. I'll miss him forever'.

An hour or so later Stephanie drove back to her office to clear up some paperwork before going back to Wayne's place where he was going to be cooking her dinner. She only had a couple of minor cases on at the moment. She didn't really want to start another major case until after Christmas so that she wasn't preoccupied whilst she was in the UK. She was already going to be missing Wayne like mad as it was.

Wayne had been asked by Patricia to take over the property management duties that had been Andy Green's job. It was a sad time for everybody but Wayne had been reluctant at first to accept Patricia's offer. He didn't want to work that closely with her given that her intention was to use him in a continuing feud with Beryl Hamilton, but he also felt a deep sense of loyalty and gratitude towards Andy's memory. So he accepted but at the same time he'd asked Stephanie to keep an eye on him and not let him fall under Patricia's manipulative influence. She'd agreed.

Since the events of that terrible afternoon Maddy hadn't mentioned again what she'd told Stephanie about before Touma al-Ashwari had gone on the rampage. If a fourth set of footprints had been found at the scene of Mariam al-Ashwari's murder then who did they belong to? And why had the evidence disappeared before suddenly reappearing again? And why had that happened now? It could all prove to be highly significant in all sorts of ways but Maddy had told Stephanie off the record and she'd no doubt forgotten all about it since which is hardly surprising considering how grief stricken she was about her Dad. So Stephanie was going to leave it for the police to sort out if they saw fit.

As far as Stephanie was concerned it was time to move on and consider this particular case closed.

Patricia opened a bottle of champagne and poured a glass each for herself and David. She took them out to the terrace of their Darling Harbour apartment and waited for David to finish on the phone to the manager of their farm.

She was slightly troubled about the file that had suddenly reappeared in the case notes relating to the events of that night three years ago. She knew that the image it contained were of her footprints. She had been there that night but she'd bolted as soon as Touma had fired her gun at Mariam. She'd stayed out of sight so that she could've surprised Neil before he noticed her lurking in the background. She'd just wanted to make him see sense. She hadn't expected it to turn out the way it had. She'd also known from her police contact that the file had found its way into the possession of Beryl Hamilton. So it must've been Beryl who'd made sure it had got back in there. She was really trying to have a go. But her safety net was that the police were hardly likely to make a connection between an anonymous set of prints and her. Why would they? There was no reason to. But she would find a way to stick the knife into Beryl. God, she'd missed the old days. It was so good to have them back.

'This looks nice' said David after he'd come through and lifted his glass. Then he sat down and clinked glasses with his wife. 'You look more relaxed than you've done in a while'.

'I think we're over the worst of the last few days, don't you?'

'You didn't get your money back from … '

' … you were going to say Neil, weren't you, darling?'

'I was but its Elaine now'.

'Well no, I didn't get my money back but I think I've got a way of getting it back through all the Ramberg accounts'.

'Is it all above board?'

'Of course it is, David. I promise you'.

'Okay, okay, just checking' said David who wished Pat had thought about how to get her money back at the start and saved them all this trouble. 'I think we should toast the champagne to Maddy Green and her recovery'.

'You're right there' said Patricia. 'And to Andy too God rest his soul'.

'To Andy. A good mate. We'll miss you'.

'But with Touma al-Answari safely behind bars the rest of us can all rest a lot easier'.

'Amen to that' said David. 'Look, Pat, I'm sorry it was Beryl who dobbed you in to the tax authorities even though you'd done nothing wrong'.

'It wasn't your fault, David'.

'I know but … well I'm just sorry that's all'.

'David, women like me are almost expected to behave with character whereas the likes of Beryl are expected to act like dried up flowers. It throws people when they go against type'.

David laughed. 'That sounded like vintage Patricia to me. But look, you will leave well alone there, won't you? I mean, you've got no schemes for retaliation forming in that pretty little head of yours?'

Patricia gave David a broad smile. 'As you often say, David, all that was a long time ago'.

THE END

Or is it?

Stephanie Marshall will be back later this year in another story that will twist around the Palmers and the Hamiltons.

AUTHOR'S NOTE

Sons and Daughters was classic eighties telly that was enjoyed by millions not just in Australia but around the world. I was in my early twenties when it came blasting onto our screens in the UK and for those of us who loved high drama it was like a penny from TV heaven. Everything seemed to revolve around the manipulative ways of Pat the Rat and the writers were clever in that you could absolutely hate her one episode and then the next you'd find yourself feeling sorry for whatever desperate state she was in. I thought it might be interesting to get back to the spirit of those early years of the show but update them with some very modern twists. I haven't written any kind of official revival book of the show. I've just used some of the characters to tell a story that they fitted nicely into. I felt it would be better if I hung their return around a new main character as the central focus. The character of Stephanie Marshall leapt out of my head one morning and onto my computer screen. She stayed there and the more I got to know her the more I liked her. She's one of the good guys but she's flawed and there's a bit of an edge to her. I thought she'd therefore fit in nicely!

I've taken a bit of a liberty with one of the main characters but the original plot line in the show was one that just didn't work for me so I decided on artistic license. The idea for this book came from a plot that had been kicking around my head for months but I couldn't find a home for it. Then it came to me. It had found its home at 'Fiona Thompson House'. I'm now planning the next book which should be out before the end of 2014. It'll be another mystery that Stephanie Marshall will be given the job of investigating but it will involve meeting up again with some more of the old characters.

I hope you have as much fun reading it as I did writing it and thank you.

David M. Paris, France. November 2013.

5405626R00115

Printed in Great Britain
by Amazon.co.uk, Ltd.,
Marston Gate.